KAT
HOT TIN
AIRSHIP

love

Sam S

KAT ON A
HOT TIN
AIRSHIP

SAM
STONE

First published in the United Kingdom in 2013 by
Telos Publishing Ltd
17 Pendre Avenue, Prestatyn, LL19 9SH

www.telos.co.uk

Telos Publishing Ltd values feedback.
Please e-mail us with any comments you may have about this
book to: feedback@telos.co.uk

ISBN: 978-1-84583-086-1

British Library Cataloguing in Publication Data.
A catalogue record for this book is available from the British
Library.

Acknowledgements

My muse: David J Howe. My publisher: Stephen James Walker. Tennessee Williams: for just being so very good at observing life.

Thanks to Keith Stephenson for designing the Perkins-Armley Purse Pistol and then for his generous gift of the weapon at The Asylum Steampunk Convivial in 2012.

Prologue

The visitor was always there. Maggie could sense him, even from an early age. There would be a strange disquiet, a sense of gathering shadows that grew around one particular corner of the nursery. It didn't bother the small child in her early years, but later, as she grew, the visitor would feel closer and she felt eyes on her all the time. Sometimes she felt like a mouse caught in an open field being circled by an owl.

As Maggie became more self-aware, puberty approached. Changes happened in her body that she felt she had no control over. Nanny Simone sat her down one day and told her what was happening. Womanhood loomed on the horizon: a terrifying future of marriage suddenly became a real possibility. Nanny Simone moved her things out of the nursery, away from her younger sister, and into a new room. A grown-up bedroom for a growing-up girl.

There was a kind of excitement and relief in moving

into the other room. This was a place of her own: no longer did she have to share any of her toys. She had a dressing table, a beautiful silver-framed mirror stood on top and Maggie watched herself as Nanny Simone brushed her long black hair one hundred times with a silver-handled brush. She could almost see the changes in her reflection. Her mouth had grown fuller. Her eyes were framed by brows that had a womanly curve. She also began to see Nanny Simone in a different light. The black nursemaid had always been there for her, but Maggie was recognising the differences between her and the house slave that had little to do with skin colour.

Her first night in her new, huge, double bed, alone in the room, was confusing and frightening. She had never slept alone before. But Nanny Simone said it was part of growing up: a relevant transition for a woman in her station.

'Leave the light on, please Nanny,' Maggie said. 'It's so dark in this room. So many dark corners.'

Nanny Simone chuckled. 'You'll get used to it, Miss Maggie.'

But she left a small oil lamp lit on the dressing table and Maggie stared at it with half-closed eyes trying to ignore the shadows that expanded either side of the room. Somehow the small light made the darkness worse.

As tiredness overwhelmed her, Maggie felt strangely homesick. She missed her sister, even though she was so much younger and often cried in the night, disturbing both of their sleep. She missed the familiar tick of the clock on the mantelpiece, the shapes of their toys scattered around the room. She felt an immense pressure inside her chest. A griping fear of the unknown. Adulthood seemed to her to be the worst thing in the world. She fell into a restless sleep, anxiety wriggling around in the back of her subconscious.

Several nights after she had moved into her new room, Maggie became aware of the visitor. She usually sensed its presence only in the nursery and she was surprised and confused to experience this feeling here. She had begun to enjoy her new bed and surroundings. The novelty, instead of waning, had become increasingly exciting. The idea of maturity was now a fascinating prospect, no longer something to fear. She had begun to value her newfound privacy. Enjoying the ability to take herself away from everything, just to be alone in her room.

Her parents were treating her differently too. Instead of ignoring her presence they occasionally addressed her. Her mother had started to give her grown-up presents. Jewellery, French perfume and sweet-smelling soaps were luxuries she had begun to enjoy and appreciate. It made her feel special and different.

She was trying on some of the jewellery – an ornate necklace, way too big and fussy for her young throat, but it made Maggie feel as though she looked like a woman already. In the mirror her reflection turned left, then right, and Maggie examined the ostentatious jewels with interest as they caught the light from the lamps.

Out of the corner of her eye she saw something dark and blurred that seemed to rush across the room. She turned her head, looking over to the curtains that hung across the big window overlooking the back of the plantation and the beds of cotton. A figure stood there. Maggie was sure of it, and she knew who it was, could smell it in the air – like the smoke from extinguished candles.

She looked away quickly. Forcing her attention back to her own image. The visitor *must* be ignored. Only then would he – and yes, Maggie always thought it was male in essence, though she never knew why – would go away. Deep down she was sure that if she acknowledged his presence she would somehow grant him the right to be there. It was like a primitive knowledge, something she instinctively understood.

She took a deep breath, but her heart pounded. She feared the shadow more than any other imagined monster and she didn't know why. It was merely a shadow! Probably all just her imagination, like Nanny Simone had said when she had tried to tell her about 'him' some years ago.

'I wonder what Nanny Simone will think of these?' Maggie whispered as though by saying the imposing nanny's name she would scare the thing away.

Her voice broke the silence, and, she hoped, disturbed the spell of uncertainty that the visitor always brought with him. Maggie stood up and turned towards the door. But the shadow was oddly dense there too. She glanced back at the window. No darkness lurked there now. It had moved – she was sure of it! She gulped in another ragged breath. Fear of something nameless – some violence she didn't understand – came up into her throat like bile.

Maggie wasn't sure what she should do. She wanted out of her room. She had to find Nanny Simone and tell her about this thing. But then, she recalled how the woman felt about what she called 'wandering imagination'. She knew she wouldn't believe her.

She sank down onto her new bed and closed her eyes. Willing the thing to go away and let her out. When she opened them again, the shadow was no longer there. Her eyes darted around the room, even as her heartbeat skipped. Then relief flooded her. It had gone again! Maybe it was some benign spirit that sometimes liked to watch the living? Maggie wasn't sure and was too afraid to tell anyone about it, for fear they would think she was going mad. Just like her Aunt Alice had all those years ago …

She ran a hand over her forehead and noted it was trembling. Her body felt weak with anxiety and she no longer wanted to be alone.

She stood, hurried to the door to her room and opened it.

A brutal face, full of demonic darkness grinned at her from the other side.

Maggie screamed.

1

New York – 1865

The creature had run from one shadow to another, as though avoiding daylight wherever it could. In outward appearance it seemed to be a middle-aged dock-worker. Wearing dusty, dark clothing that had seen better days. A flat cap, pulled down over his eyes, covered thinning hair. He was to the casual eye an ordinary man. Quite invisible to anyone of note.

I perhaps wouldn't have noticed him at all but for the bulky sack he carried. It looked too large and heavy for one person to bear, yet the man hefted it with little trouble. His bulging muscles barely registered the weight as he slung the straps over his back and hurried away towards the row of warehouses near the dock. I knew then that he wasn't what he appeared to be.

Keeping well back, and abandoning my plans to meet

up with George Pepper and Martin Crewe in Battery Park, I followed.

There was a row of secure warehouses on the dock, and the nervous man hurried past a stack of empty crates that had been abandoned just outside the first structure. He paused, looking back, as though some supernatural sense told him he was being followed. I ducked down behind a mound of broken pieces of wood, and waited there until I was certain he had moved on.

By the time I looked around the heap, he had passed the first warehouse and was headed towards a doorway in the side of the second. I carried on then, pausing by the crates just as he had.

I placed my reticule on top of one of the crates, looked around, and then quickly unfastened the long skirt that would only delay me. After tripping over a dress and almost being ripped to shreds by a horde of demons out for blood, I'd learnt the hard way that female clothing wasn't conducive to my line of work. So, I wore a pair of tight breeches and calf-length flat-heeled boots underneath my formal clothing for these sort of occasions.

I opened my reticule and retrieved my weapons belt. On it hung a hand-held clockwork crossbow, the holster for a Crewe-Remington Laser, which when armed was connected to a wrist holster that contained a power pack that provided energy for the weapon when the sun was down, or when needed inside. The weapon itself stored a small amount of power but wasn't good for prolonged use without the pack.

Martin Crewe had designed this gun for me, after his initial prototype worked so well some years before when the shop in which we worked, Tiffany & Co, was besieged by zombies. The failure of the previous model had always been its limitation to daylight use. Martin had harvested that power since. The weapon now lay inside the pack, and all I had to do to charge it was to leave it on the ledge by my window for a day. The sun was sucked inside by a small panel containing a module rigged with what Martin called 'electronic' wires. It somehow absorbed natural light and conducted it down the wires to operate the system. Martin called it a SunPan. Somehow this clever device captured and stored the energy and used it to power the gun. It meant that I could use it anywhere now, even in the darkest room.

I stuffed my brown velvet skirt behind the back of the crates, strapped the belt around my waist, the holster on my thigh, and the wrist holster around my right wrist. On my other thigh I added another holster. This one contained an adapted Colt 45. Instead of firing ordinary bullets the Colt now fired shells containing liquid nitrogen. The bullets were dangerous – guaranteed to explode on impact – fortunately my clever friend Martin had coated the bullets with a benign substance that kept the content cold and stable until they met with the warmer flesh of the target.

I pulled on a pair of leather gloves, removed the bullets from a metal cartridge and began to load them into the gun. It took six in all. And six were usually more than enough to deal with any enemy.

I patted my ankle, making sure that the knife hidden there was still secure. It was made of steel and silver and encrusted with diamond shards. Hard. Deadly. And of course we had learnt in the last few years that silver and diamonds were poison to a lot of the things I fought. Yes, I was armed to the teeth. And weapons were something I had come to rely on in the fight against the Darkness, an unstoppable evil that used it's many minions to try to destroy the goodness in humanity.

I guess some would say the Darkness was the devil, and that the demons came from hell. Maybe they did, and I supposed that these things had been around for the whole history of mankind, which explained where the many superstitions of heaven and hell came from. In my case I had found hypocrisy in organised religion and, although I had every reason to believe that there was certainly an evil out there waiting in the dark ready to manipulate man, I was somewhat cynical about the idea of a 'god'. I had good reason to be. All I saw in our city was evil, and I was fighting every day to push it back. To stop it from consuming us all, plunging the world into a dark pit that would never be salvageable. That was why, if I saw even one of those things living among mankind, I killed it on sight.

The Darkness was an infection. It was a leech. It fed on our misery, making itself stronger.

And me? I'm Kat Lightfoot. Fighting the evil brought into the world by the Darkness was just an average day in New York. And so, I hid my reticule with the skirt behind the crates and slid along the wall, careful to remain unobserved.

I reached the side door of the second warehouse, now armed and ready for the battle I would probably face.

Inside I quickly merged with the dark, hiding behind the nearest row of boxes. The warehouse was unusually dark and quiet. I could make out shapes of cartons, crates, pallets of goods, all stacked in neat rows. I had not expected it to be bustling, not if this thing were hiding out here. Humans tended to avoid them, even when they didn't know why. A natural dislike of the creatures … or maybe we had all developed another sense since the first uprising, I wasn't sure. Most people, however, went about their daily life oblivious to the demons and monsters walking among them. I think I'd once been the same before my eyes were opened and New York nearly fell to the Darkness. That day we had been saved by our domestic cats, which had been carrying a venom in their claws that was deadly to the zombies and an effective cure for anyone newly-infected. The infection had spread too quickly, we were outnumbered. Without the cats we would have been doomed for certain.

Since then, though, the battle had continued, and Pepper, Martin and I were seemingly the only people who knew how to fight back when the things got greedy and came out of their hiding places again.

Something scurried across the aisle. I cocked the laser pistol, removed the safety, and switched on the battery. Then I looked down the sight, scanned the dark area and stepped out from behind the crates.

I took a few quiet steps, glanced down another crossroad of crates, then moved on. There was a strange chattering sound, like the faint twitter of crickets on a hot night. *Interesting.* I moved forward, with slow intent, checking the rows each time I reached an intersection. The layout reminded me of the Manhattan City grid, and I began to treat each section as a block that would take me closer to the target.

One step further on and the chattering, chirruping noise became louder. I glanced down the next aisle. Nothing there, but I was rapidly approaching an open space in the centre of the warehouse that could be dangerously exposed for me. As I edged towards the end of the rows, something moved across the bottom. I ducked back behind the nearest row of boxes. The chattering stopped. I held my breath, afraid I'd been heard, but after a moment the sound resumed, only this time I could also hear the scamper of feet ahead. It sounded like the scrape of thousands of insects, skittering across a wooden floor.

I peeped around the boxes, saw there was no-one there, then edged forward again. At the end of the row I looked into the gloom of the warehouse. Dull light filtered in from skylight windows above, casting the occasional spotlight glow down into the large, empty space. It was a dullish day out, perfect weather to encourage Darkness creatures to venture out. They were rarely ever found in bright sunlight.

I saw the one I had followed, placing his stolen wares down on the floor in the centre. From this distance it still appeared human, but experience had taught me that you couldn't take anyone at face value anymore. The sound of chirruping grew louder, and then I saw other things creep from the shadows, out towards the sack of stolen food the thing had brought them.

They were beings of the Darkness for sure. An ancient demon, three-legged, vile, with grey slime-covered skin, was moving faster than the rest towards the spoils. The smell of putrefaction wafted from his skin. I pressed my free hand over my nose to prevent the stench from making me gag. Another monster, disguised as an urchin, hobbled forward. Its flesh bulged with poison-filled boils. I felt a vague rush of sympathy for the urchin whose body had been stolen. He had probably been alive when they took him. But the demons cared nothing for human life, and the bodies they used were no longer fit for human souls to inhabit. The best I could do for this one now was kill the body, sending the demon straight back to whatever 'hell' it came from. Hopefully freeing the tortured human soul if it was still trapped inside: an issue of uncertainty that my colleagues and I had often debated upon.

I waited for all of the creatures to gather, to be sure that none was waiting in the shadows.

The chirruping sound picked up, and I realised with surprise that this was some form of private language they had. The demons I had conversed with usually spoke in English before I killed them. I guess it hadn't occurred to me until now that this was all part of the mimicking process.

The dock-worker demon bent down and opened the large bag it had brought. There were some 15 or 20 of them gathered now, and you have to pick your battles carefully. I was beginning to think that retreat would be the best course of action this time. All well and good taking one or two down, but this seemed too many. I was alone, possibly didn't have enough weaponry to finish them all, and it was likely that the creatures would turn nasty as soon as one of them was destroyed. I looked from one to the other, trying to work out exactly what they were. You see, not all monsters are the same. Some are demons, others zombies, some are shades. There are nephilims, and phantoms. All carnivorous in their own way … These appeared to be … *skinners* … which meant that the package would contain …

A small cry emerged from the sack. I had been right! There was a baby inside and it was screaming its lungs out, while a mother somewhere was undoubtedly mourning the loss of her child.

The condition of the bodies made more sense now. The demons were losing their grip on them, the human tissue was rejecting the evil inside – hence the boils, lesions and smell of rot. They could no longer pass as human. This was a desperate time for them.

I had to act. If I left now the child would be killed, its lifeforce used to rejuvenate the bodies the skinners had stolen and were wearing like old clothes. These warped and twisted creatures were hoping to save their pelts. To mend them, like crudely stitched rags, so that they could once again merge with the populace. They would appear as beggars, urchins, sweeps, factory and dock-workers. The type of humans that people treated as invisible and would barely spend time scrutinising. And they would do this by skinning the flesh from a newborn, each consuming a piece: the only way to restore this kind

18

of demon's power. Or so it was rumoured. I didn't know for certain, because I had never come across one before. I just recalled hearing about them from a water demon I despatched some time ago.

We had coerced some truths out of the thing before we killed it. He had told us about nephilims, water nymphs – something sailors called sirens – and skinners.

Skinners *were* different from the usual demons and cross-breeds, because they borrowed bodies to live in. At the time I hadn't believed him when he'd described the awful ritual they performed to sustain themselves. I had thought the demon had been lying to save his own life, but obviously he had told the truth.

The group drew closer to their meal, and now I saw vicious claws and fanged teeth as the glamour that hid their true nature dropped, warping the stolen bodies into animalistic changelings. I had to do something! It was foolhardy, but I would act regardless: I couldn't stand here and let the child die.

'Back away from the kid,' I said, stepping out from behind my hiding place.

The creatures rounded on me immediately. Gaping maws snapped vicious, shark-like teeth. Black eyes took in my weapons, and the one I had followed – possibly their leader – began to laugh in that awful chirruping way.

'You are no match for us, girl!' Its voice was a breathy hiss. 'But we know of you. You and your companions …'

Its face, though still mostly human, was showing signs of wear and tear. Soon none of them would be able to blend in, so they were all as desperate as they could be. And desperate meant extremely dangerous when survival was the ultimate prize.

I was pointing the gun on instinct. Taking this one out first might help, but I didn't know what type of weapon would work best.

'I'm not alone,' I bluffed, hoping they really did know of me and my companions. 'This whole place is surrounded.'

The creatures looked around nervously. The chittering started up again and a furious row seemed to take place between the dock-worker demon and the urchin with the pustules.

The urchin looked over at me, assessing my nerves to see if I was bluffing. But I'd learnt to keep my poker face in place some years ago. And I *always* had a steady hand, even though I felt that familiar rush of fear and excitement that normally came before a fight.

'We are only trying to survive ...' said the urchin.

Its face now looked cherubic, pustules hidden, I knew, behind a wall of their hypnotic glamour. He was an adorable child. I could see why the demon had chosen this body to inhabit. He could hide safely inside, while the unsuspecting mortals around him patted his innocent-looking head and fed him crumbs from their own tables.

I blinked away the glamour spell with little hesitation. That kind of simple magic required the person to be complicit in receiving it. I wasn't, and therefore, could not be fooled. The face of the urchin returned to the bloated plague-covered mass it had been.

'Nice try kid, or whatever you are. I'm not taken in

by parlour tricks. Now back away from the baby. I won't ask nicely again.'

The urchin glanced back at the other skinners and barked a chattering order. They backed away.

'Not too far. I want you all to stay where I can see you,' I warned.

'But why do you even care?' said the urchin. 'If we take this one life, then 20 others will be spared.'

'What are you talking about?'

'We have to survive, just as you do. These bodies are deteriorating. We need to repair them, or take new ones. One life … this baby … will spare many others.'

'I'm not letting you eat that child, skinner,' I warned.

There was a collective gasp as the creatures reacted to the knowledge I held about them.

'You think you *know* what we are?' said the urchin.

And yes he was beginning to annoy me in the way most arrogant demons always do.

'I know what you are, and how you obtained those bodies. Back away from the child or I'm going to ensure that that body won't be any use to any of you anymore.'

The urchin feigned backing away as I knew he would. He turned as though to go, then dived back towards the crying child. I fired the laser gun, severing the clawed hand that reached out for the baby's delicate flesh.

The skinner-urchin gave a satisfying scream and fell back onto the floor, clutching his maimed arm. It was good to know that they would feel pain, but I had little time to think about it as the other skinners used the distraction to sink back into the shadows and disappear, leaving the urchin and the dock-worker. Both of whom were unwilling to abandon their prize.

I now had a dilemma. I could kill the two remaining and try to take the baby, but I was certain that the other skinners were circling around the warehouse in an attempt to cut off my exit.

I had no time to waste. I blasted the laser into the face of the urchin, which exploded in a mass of blood, pus, skull and brain. I then arched the beam over to the rapidly retreating dock-worker and caught him as he reached the edge of darkness. The laser lit up the corner, exploding into his back, sending him smashing face first into a pile of crates. The boxes tumbled and scattered with the force of the bulky, now dead, body that crashed into them. I heard the chattering spreading all around me. I could wait for them to come at me, one at a time, while protecting the child, or I could take my chances and try to get back to the door I had entered.

I hurried to the sack, pushed aside the severed hand of the urchin and lifted the baby out of the middle. The sack was filled with all kinds of spoils – tools, food, clothing – hence the bulk of it. The baby was wrapped in a thin blanket. He looked bruised but mostly unharmed. I lifted him up and tucked him in my left arm, while scanning the area for possible attack.

A burst of chittering filled the air. I stood up, gun ready, and made my way cautiously back to the stack of crates, and the shadows that hid my waiting foe.

Once in my arms the child hushed its constant sobbing,

as though he knew he was safe for now. I passed the first aisle without incident, but rushed onwards because now I felt speed was more essential than stealth.

A skinner burst out from behind a pallet containing canned food. It caught my leather-gloved hand, severed the connection to the power pack and knocked the laser clear of my fingers. I heard the gun fall to the floor, skidding off somewhere to the left. I ducked as the skinner swung its clawed fingers at my head, then holding tight to the baby, I dived between two rows of crates. I switched arms, pulling out the Colt 45, grateful that I'd had the foresight to load it before entering the warehouse. The skinner was soon behind me and I pulled the gun up to face him, just as a second skinner dived down into the gap between us from the crates above. The gun went off into the chest of the nearest demon, blasting a hole through him. The skinner's body exploded backwards, taking out the demon behind him as the blast burst from the back of the first, into the chest of the second. The carcasses crashed back into the pallet of tin cans.

The air was rank with the smell of burnt demon and rot as the bodies, sustained long beyond their natural death, now rapidly fell into total decay.

The baby was crying loudly again: I made no effort to hush it. There wasn't any point; the skinners knew exactly where we were.

I weaved through the crates, as cautious as was possible in the circumstances. All I needed to do was get outside: the skinners were unlikely to follow in their current condition.

I saw the door, light filtered in around the edges as it was slightly ajar. Maybe the row had raised the alarm and someone else had come in? I hoped not. Another civilian to save would be an inconvenience. I paused. It could be a trap, of course. The skinners may have opened the door to encourage me to rush forward, taking less care, while they gathered at the sides waiting to pick me off.

The baby had quieted. I glanced down at him, noted with surprise that he had fallen asleep. Then I felt the heavy breath of a demon standing right behind me. I threw myself aside, smashing into a pile of empty crates, that tumbled over with the impact – less dramatic that the earlier fall of full crates as the urchin and dock-worker died, but no less useful because as I knocked over the crates, I immediately ducked away to the other side of the aisle. By that time the clumsy skinner had thrown itself forward, and now it fell down onto the floor at my feet. I pulled the trigger of the gun and blew the bastard back to hell. It was very cathartic.

I ran for the door as it opened wide before me. Daylight poured in, blinding me momentarily before my eyes could adjust from the gloom. A shape loomed, outlined by the light, shadow large. It lifted something it was carrying and swung. Then I noticed that a skinner had been running almost parallel to me down the aisle to my right. The creature fell at my feet, head crushed by the handle on a very familiar cane ... a cat's head made from silver ...

George Pepper pulled out the hidden sword from inside the cane and pierced the prone body for good measure.

24

'When I heard the explosions I knew you were in trouble,' Pepper said as he pulled me and the baby out of the warehouse.

He slammed the door shut as a skinner crashed against it in a last-ditch attempt to snatch back the prize. Then Pepper wedged a piece of shattered crate into the handle to prevent it being opened from inside.

2

'We have to blow this place,' I said.

'Lucky for you I have this then,' said Pepper, showing me a stick of dynamite. He had several more sticks in a bag by his feet.

'I'm blessed to have such a useful friend,' I said.

'What's with the kid?' Pepper asked.

'Skinners ...'

'Ah,' said Pepper, catching on immediately to the importance of the devastation needed.

The door heaved behind us. Pepper leaned on it.

'Just one problem,' I said. 'I don't think that dynamite will be enough to bring this place down.'

Pepper looked down at the pack and nodded.

'But I have something inside my reticule that could boost it.'

I hurried back to my hiding place, pulled free the

26

reticule, and wrapped the baby in my skirt to cushion him from the sounds of explosion that would soon occur if the plan I was formulating worked out well. I then laid him inside one of the open crates.

'You should be safe here for the time being,' I said. The baby slept on as though he knew now he was completely safe. I hoped for his sake that the door held out until we could prepare the dynamite.

I took my reticule back to the doorway. Then we began the process of pressing the nitrogen bullets into the sticks.

'Good thinking,' Pepper said.

'The dangerous part will be lighting them, opening this door and throwing them inside without allowing the skinners to escape.'

'I have an idea,' Pepper said.

Pepper's idea sounded insane and dangerous. He planned to climb up on the roof, enter the warehouse through the skylight windows, and then to distract the skinners long enough to allow me to enter by the door. Then between us we would place the bombs at various points in the warehouse. Once the dynamite was lit though, we didn't have much time to get out again. It would rely on us both making our way back to the door, and out again before the whole thing blew.

'I can't imagine you climbing up onto the roof with your bad leg,' I pointed out. 'I'll have to do it. But instead of going inside, why don't we just drop the bombs through the skylights?'

'It won't be as accurate, or as devastating to the structure as placing them directly under the support beams will be.'

Pepper drew a map in the dirt with the tip of his sword.

'This is where the bombs need to be placed,' he said. Indicating where he thought the support walls and beams of the building were most likely to be. 'From what you say, they die fairly easily. Bringing the structure down on their heads might just be enough to finish the whole lot of them.'

'Their weakness is the human bodies they've decided to live in. Bodies that can still be injured or killed and I've discovered that they feel pain. Which is always a bonus.'

We argued for a moment about who would take the chance on entering and as always I won. Pepper couldn't run as fast as I could, due to his injury, and I already knew the layout of the warehouse.

'Keep them by the door until I've placed the bombs,' I said.

I cut down some of the fuses on the dynamite, and lengthened those on the others. Then I removed a further roll of fuse that was in my reticule, tying it to my belt.

'When you hear the first commotion, get the door freed but leave it closed. I'll yell when I'm near.'

I made my way silently across the roof. I was carrying a sack containing the bombs, and had a long length of rope coiled over my shoulder. I glanced down the first skylight and noted a cluster of skinners pounding on the door. We had already made sure that they couldn't escape by any other route. Fortunately the huge warehouse doors overlooking the dock were held together by a heavy chain to protect the contents from potential thieves. The skinners must have known this, as they had made no attempt to leave this way. The only way out was through the side door, and Pepper had this blocked.

I walked to the back of the warehouse, stopping at points to look down. I could see the clearing and the bodies of the dock-worker and urchin still there along with the carnage I'd left behind after exploding the other skinners. None of them had attempted to move the decaying bodies, which meant that they were all too focused on their own survival now. Making this particularly dangerous for Pepper and I.

I opened the skylight closest to the back of the warehouse. There was a beam crossing the centre of the building, just below the window. I lowered myself in and onto it. Then tied the rope around the beam, quietly lowering it down into the warehouse. I squinted down into the dark. It looked long enough, but I wasn't sure if it reached the bottom. I would just have to take the chance.

I slid onto the rope, wrapping one leg around it for extra support, then shimmied downwards as silently as possible.

I heard the chittering of the skinners, but it sounded far away. As I reached the end of the rope, I realised it didn't quite stretch down as far as I would have liked. I looked down. It was maybe ten feet from the ground, but I had jumped down further distances in the past with only a few scrapes. The problem here of course would be the noise I'd make. I wasn't ready to attract attention just yet. I needed to do that on my terms when the first bombs were in place.

I slid down the rope as far as possible, then let go,

landing with a soft thud, and a roll, to try and prevent injury and noise. As I landed the skinner chatter peaked and grew louder. I heard Pepper banging on the door to aggravate them, and blessed his timing. My slight thump went unnoticed and I hurried off towards the first corner and quickly placed the first bomb.

After that, moving around the warehouse was easy. I kept low, placed the bombs, joining them all to the long fuse that I would light as soon as the skinners became aware of my presence.

I retraced my steps from earlier, heading back towards the door, wire falling between the aisles of crates, in a way I hoped the skinners wouldn't notice until it was too late. Then I found myself back near the pallet of tin cans. I picked one up, weighing it in my hand.

The time had come to draw them away from the door. I threw the can over the crates to one of the corners furthest away from me, and nowhere near any of the bombs.

The skinner chatter halted. I threw another can. Then sank back behind the pallet and waited as two skinners hurried past towards the area I had thrown the cans. I lit the fuse and moved away, but first loaded a few more cans into the now almost empty sack. I had one more bomb to place near the door, and for that the skinners would all have to be drawn away. I began tossing the cans in various directions away from myself. Then circled the area that the skinners had previously searched which was easy because they made no attempt to hide themselves. I reached the door to find that two of the creatures remained.

I was hoping that Pepper had silently removed the cane from the handle and I would be able to make a quick exit, but the two skinners were blocking my way. I had the Colt 45, but the blasts from the bullets would most likely bring the rest of the creatures running back. That was the last thing I needed. I made my way back towards the stack of cans, and as I refilled the sack two skinners turned the corner and headed towards the pallet. I ducked down before they saw me, then crawled across the row towards another aisle. My hand fell on something cold. It was the barrel of a gun. My Crewe-Remington Laser was once more in my hands. I was no longer wearing the battery pack, thinking the gun lost, but I hoped that it still had enough energy to work one final time for me.

I hurried back towards the door, weaving in and out of the rows to avoid contact with the searching monsters. Time was running out. The fuse was lit and this whole place was due to go up any second.

As I reached the door, the first explosion went off at the back of the warehouse. The building shook and the two skinners blocking my exit looked around surprised.

'Pepper, open the door!' I yelled as I barrelled out from behind the crates and ran full pelt towards the creatures. I aimed the laser and pulled the trigger, a burst of light poured from the gun, striking at the eyes of one of the skinners. He fell aside, blinded and screaming. The other threw himself sideways away from the door as I rushed forward.

I lit the final bomb as I ran. Its fuse was so short I knew

I would just have time to drop it and run but so far Pepper hadn't opened the door. I glanced over my shoulder. More than six of the skinners were making their way back towards me. I ran full pelt, dropped the bomb and tugged the door just as Pepper opened it.

I fell out, tumbling to my knees on the floor. Pepper slammed the door shut, grabbed my arm and lifted me up. Though winded, I ran as fast as my legs could carry me, and was astounded as Pepper half-hobbled, half-ran, refusing to let his bad leg hold us up. We reached the stack of empty crates where I had hidden the baby and I scooped him up, ducking down as the warehouse went up in a series of explosions.

Pepper, ever the gentleman, threw himself over the baby and I, shielding us from a spray of glass that rained down from the roof windows.

I heard the yawn and groan as the timber beams gave in and the old building stumbled and fell as the support collapsed in on itself.

Pepper jumped up with more agility than he should have, and rushed back to the building to ensure that none of the skinners had escaped.

I looked down at the little baby in my arms and I could have sworn he was smiling in his sleep.

3

New Orleans: A Few Months Later

The train rattled along the tracks. Steam and smoke blew past the window of our first class carriage. Mother had been pleased that we were able to afford one, and not have to mix with the 'rabble' outside. We were on the final leg of the journey after travelling for three days, with two overnight stops.

'How much longer?' my kid sister Sally whined. She was thirteen and had become even more difficult recently.

'We're almost there,' Mother said. 'Have a lemon drop ...'

Mother had been feeding her candy for the last hour and Pepper had been trying his best to entertain her by performing a few card tricks he had learnt in his army days. I was impressed with him because it was obvious that the journey was taking its toll, and his old war wound was causing him discomfort.

'Why don't we stretch our legs a little?' I suggested.

'That's a great idea,' Pepper said. He winced as he stood, but he followed me, reticule and all, out into the train corridor.

'I propose we walk down to the dining car and back …' I said. 'That should help relieve some of the fatigue.'

It had been a trying journey for us all, especially as Mother wasn't too impressed that George Pepper had insisted on coming with us, and I had done little to discourage him.

'Don't be long, dear,' Mother said as Pepper turned to close the door behind us.

Mother didn't quite understand how Pepper and I could spend so much time together yet have no romantic interest in each other. Mother, of course, hadn't seen the things that we had seen. She saw that Pepper was an attractive man, with his pale blond hair and bright blue eyes. His soldier's physique and sharp wit would probably appeal to most women. But he and Martin were my trusted friends and colleagues in a way that Mother couldn't relate to and thought was inappropriate.

I didn't want her to know the full facts of how I now earned my living even though I think she knew on a subconscious level. She quite literally turned a blind eye when I left the house dressed as a man. Breeches where so much more practical than a wide skirt when you were chasing down a banshee, or scaring off a demon dressed as a little boy. And she never questioned the frequent visits I made to the police station. Nor the odd telegraphs I received from Inspector Stark asking me for urgent assistance. On those occasions, I would rush upstairs, change, arm up, and then call next door for Pepper. The two of us would hail a cab and disappear for hours, often returning dirty, bedraggled and with a pouch full of money.

Even so, being funded by the police to rid the city of these pests would only remain lucrative while the demons were around. Although I sometimes wished that we had seen the last of them, and I could take a 'normal' job to support Mother and Sally, I knew that I would miss the action and adrenaline that had become so important to my survival. Somehow I doubted that I would be able to work and live in a way that would be deemed 'normal' now.

Pepper and I moved along the narrow corridor towards the buffet car. As we walked his limp became less pronounced and he stopped wincing and I realised that stretching out was helping him a great deal. His injury had improved a lot over the last few years, and although he would never walk completely without a hobble, he had certainly improved his ability to run.

We opened the door and stepped out onto the short bridge between the cars. The rush of air from the moving train felt wonderful. The closer we got to New Orleans, the more the temperature rose. It was late October and so the continued heat was something of a surprise to me. I held onto the railing and looked out over the land either side of the track, breathing in the warm air, feeling the rush of the wind, while Pepper stared out of the other side.

'Almost there,' I said, a feeling of anticipation fuelling the strange enthusiasm I felt for the trip.

'This will be a well earned rest for us all,' Pepper said.

'Yes,' I nodded. 'I know.'

The door to the buffet car opened and a striking young man came out. I leaned back against the rail as he went to pass me. Then his eyes met mine and I gasped. They were a bright amber in colour and I had only ever seen eyes like this once before: he was nephilim.

'Excuse me, Miss' he said politely.

I was too surprised to react, and it was too public a place to despatch the creature without drawing attention to ourselves.

He frowned a little as he noticed my scrutiny. He was dressed as any Southern gentleman might be. Smart breeches in grey, a pristine white shirt under a long black jacket, and a wide-brimmed hat to shade his face from the sun.

'Are you alright?' he drawled, running his finger over his handle-bar moustache as though he felt that this might be the cause of my shocked expression.

I wasn't all right. I felt *strange*. A previous neph that I had encountered had told me things about the underworld in an attempt to save his life. He had also told me that not all nephs knew what they were. That didn't mean they weren't evil though. I wondered if this neph knew his identity, or whether he truly believed he was the Southern gentleman he appeared to be.

'Kat?' said Pepper behind the neph.

The man turned. 'Good day, Sir,' he said. 'Your lady seems to be feeling a little …'

Pepper drew in a breath as he caught sight of the man's eyes.

'Let me introduce myself. I'm Orlando Pollitt.' The neph held out his hand to Pepper. 'And believe me I'm used to that reaction to my eyes, so no need to be embarrassed.'

Pepper shook Pollitt's hand warily while I regained my senses. I had been momentarily lost in the beauty of his eyes, especially the kindness that seemed to be in them. I was intrigued and my natural instinct to maim and kill anything remotely linked to the Darkness was completely numbed.

'Pollitt …?' I stammered. 'Are you any relation to Margaret Pollitt?'

'Why yes … that's my sister,' Orlando said.

Pepper and I exchanged glances.

'I'm Katherine Lightfoot,' I said, quickly regaining my composure. 'And this is my colleague, Mr George Pepper. Your sister married my brother, Henry, and we are travelling to visit and take part in the festivities.'

Maybe Orlando had no clue that he was a cross-breed. He had been brought up, I hoped, in a normal family environment. Although I wouldn't know that until I reached the plantation and took stock of the Pollitts. You see nephilims aren't just demons. They are the result of an unholy coupling, of a demon male with a human female, which meant that Orlando's mother had been seduced by one. She may not even know that her child was different. But all of this raised the question of the wife my brother had chosen. Could it be that my brother Henry had married the offspring of a demon?

'Why, that's wonderful!' Orlando said. 'I didn't realise that Henry Lightfoot had such a darling lady for a sister. This is going to be so much more fun that I had ever imagined it would be. Welcome to New Orleans, Miss Lightfoot, Mr Pepper. It's great to have you folks here.'

I was tired from the journey and Mother and Sally's impatience, but it wasn't like me to be so confused by a demon. Demon blood meant 'evil' as far as I was concerned, but I wasn't getting Darkness vibes from Orlando. My reaction to him was quite the reverse and I was sure that Pepper was feeling the same. And he really was rather lovely to look at. He looked angelic, not demonic. But then I recalled the urchin in the warehouse. Perhaps Orlando was using some form of glamour? I blinked several times, but my vision didn't alter, in fact the more I looked at him, the more attractive he appeared to be. Even so, I could see no evidence at all of magic.

'You must come and meet my mother and sister,' I found myself saying.

I ignored the frown that appeared on Pepper's brow as I led Orlando back to our car. But I knew he didn't know how to react to Orlando either. Plus, what else was I going to do? I couldn't just kill the brother of Henry's new wife, in public, for no apparent reason. Particularly when he seemed so normal.

A few minutes later, soon after the introductions were made, the train pulled into the station.

As we climbed from the carriage, Orlando was greeted by a tall black man.

'Why, Mister Orlando! You back. We weren't expecting you for a day or two.'

'I suspect you're here to collect these good folks then,

Isaac?' said Orlando.

'Mrs Lightfoot?' Isaac said nodding. 'Oh yes, Sir. Big Daddy and Big Momma is looking forward to meeting them ...'

'This is incredible,' said Mother as Orlando sent Isaac to organise two carriages. I could see that all of her concerns about the trip were being laid to rest by the charm Orlando exuded. Both she and Sally were calmer than they had been since the start of the journey, or indeed since we received the letter telling us of Henry's elopement.

We climbed into an open top carriage that Isaac brought to take us all to the Pollitt Plantation, while our luggage was loaded onto a hired cart.

'Let me take that bag for you, Miss Katherine,' said Orlando.

'That's fine, I prefer to carry this one myself,' I said.

Orlando looked confused, but allowed me to hold onto my carpet bag without further comment. Demons were good at pretending to be people, and although Orlando appeared to be genuinely unaware of his heritage, I wasn't going to take any chances with Mother and Sally's lives.

'Kat!' said Sally rudely as she climbed up into the carriage. 'What's with his eyes?'

The carriage afforded us a cool breeze, and Orlando was charming Mother almost as much as Sally, who had become uncharacteristically shy around him.

Orlando had seated me in the back, facing our journey and had placed Mother and Sally opposite. Then he sat down beside me, leaving Pepper no choice but to sit next to Mother. He was nearest the carriage down on my right and so directly opposite me. I had placed the carpet bag down at my feet between us for ease of access.

'What a charming family you have,' Orlando said to Mother. 'And two lovely daughters ...' at which Sally blushed redder than I had ever seen her. 'But I don't understand who ...?'

'Oh, Pepper? He is my friend,' I said.

Orlando's eyes scrutinised us both as Mother looked away embarrassed. She would of course find Pepper very difficult to explain this week. Unlike if we were betrothed. But I'd had too many arguments with her, trying to explain that this was unlikely to ever happen.

'So you two are ...?' Orlando said.

'Good heavens no!' I said. 'We are *just* friends. Pepper is practically family though ...'

'Why, that's mighty interesting to hear ...' Orlando said and his smile implied that he was very pleased indeed.

It was now my turn to blush. I looked away, straight into the eyes of Pepper. He appeared pale compared to the darker, sun-seared skin of Orlando. His blue eyes were confused, hurt. It made me feel strange inside. There was a dull ache in my stomach at the thought that I had somehow upset him. Pepper was my dearest friend. He had saved my life on more occasions than I could recall. I mulled over what had been said, and couldn't figure out what might have upset him. Maybe it was just this close proximity to the nephilim? It certainly confused and disturbed me.

SAM STONE

At that moment the carriage went over a bump and I was jostled, and almost thrown off my seat. Orlando caught me around the waist and held me way longer than was appropriate. I pulled away and sat back more securely in the seat. When I was resettled I looked across at Mother and noticed she was smiling very broadly at Orlando. There was an interesting expression on her face that I couldn't read. She liked him. He *was* charming. And I could feel a strange tingling warmth around my waist where his hands had been.

'Miss Katherine,' Orlando said. 'If you just look over this way you can see my family's plantation. It's a few miles away yet, but we are now on Pollitt land.'

He leaned closer, pointing towards a huge white building on the horizon. I could smell his masculine cologne.

'Stunning!' I said.

'Yes,' Orlando breathed, and I felt that same blush blooming once more on my cheeks as I glanced back and found he was looking at me, and not the house on the horizon. Orlando made me feel peculiar. His interest both flattered and embarrassed me. It made me feel somewhat like an ordinary girl, and not the demon-slayer that I knew I was.

A short way up we came across a row of huts, each fronted by a short porch. There were several black men busily working around the huts. One was up a ladder and was hammering a wooden facia back in place, while another man was painting the front walls with a dark wood stain.

'What's this?' asked Mother.

'These are the workers' homes,' said Orlando. 'Big

41

Daddy has given them leave to make some improvements.'

'They aren't slaves are they?' blurted Sally.

'Miss Sally,' said Orlando. 'Everyone on Pollitt land is a free man or woman. We were already making changes here, long before the war. Isn't that right Isaac?'

Isaac was sat in the front of the carriage, next to the driver and he turned in his seat to look back at us.

'Yes Sir, Mister Orlando. That's why there's so many people still here working. Pollitt Plantation has housed freed-slaves for many years. We work here for a living, like white folks do.'

'That's really admirable …' Pepper said, breaking the silence he had maintained so far.

'Why thank you Mr Pepper,' said Orlando. 'Fortunately our radical thinking made things easier for us on Pollitt Plantation than most folks in these parts. Which is why my Momma and Daddy are so happy to welcome y'all and to have such a kind man marry into the family.'

'Henry is kind,' I said. 'I'm looking forward to seeing him. We haven't seen him now for several years, even though he has always maintained contact by letter.'

The carriage continued on, but inside I was wondering what this visit might bring.

4

The main house was indeed impressive. An imposing mansion with whitewashed walls that gleamed in the sunshine. Two grand staircases extended upwards to the entrance at either side of the large front door. Orlando led us up the steps on the left and the door opened as though by some will of its own. A row of servants lined the entrance hall of a magnificent hallway. A cream coloured marble floor gave way to an even more striking central staircase that led upwards to a first landing, then split in two to cover either side of a balcony that traversed the entire hallway. Doors and rooms led off the balcony, as did, I soon learnt, corridors that serviced wings stretching out right and left of the house.

Either side of the hallway were two sets of doors, and two further corridors that led away to other rooms, cloning the landings above.

'My!' said Mother as she stepped over the threshold.

She didn't have to say more than that. I understood completely what she was feeling. None of us had ever seen such an impressive house before. It was so big that I was certain we could get lost inside in it if we weren't careful to mark our direction.

'This is a large house,' Orlando said, reading our minds. 'Probably not such a good idea to wander off alone until you know your way around.'

He looked at Sally while he spoke, but I felt that the warning was addressed to us all. It made me feel slightly uncomfortable. As though this meant that the many corridors and rooms held secrets which we were not going to be made privy to. Of course this was understandable in the circumstances. We were strangers, even if Henry had married into the family. We were also Northerners. And I was certain there would be some prejudices hidden behind the welcoming smiles. It was only to be expected.

'The Lightfoots, I presume!' said a voice from above.

I looked up to see an attractive woman of similar age to Mother, but wealth and privilege made her appear much younger. She was wearing the most daring dress I had ever seen. The pale green skirt was wide, something you might wear to a ball, rather than every day. Her shoulders were bare, and she wore a large, bulky necklace made up of red and green jewels. It could have been paste jewellery – it was so ostentatious – but I was certain that the jewels were genuine rubies and emeralds set in solid gold.

'Momma,' said Orlando. 'It is my absolute pleasure

to present Mrs Lightfoot and her charming daughters, Miss Katherine and Miss Sally.'

'How marvellous!' said Mrs Pollitt as she swept down the stairs.

She went straight to Mother and hugged her as though she were an old friend, then she moved onto me and Sally. She stood confused when she came face to face with Pepper.

'Henry never said he had a brother ...' Mrs Pollitt said.

Orlando took his mother's arm and explained the situation with Pepper, who gallantly bent over her offered hand and kissed her bejewelled fingers.

'Mr Pepper felt we needed an escort to travel this far from home ...' Mother said.

'Well you are most welcome also Mr Pepper,' she said smiling at him flirtatiously. 'We hardly ever see a handsome face around here, that is ... none that aren't related to us!'

'Mrs Pollitt,' Mother said, 'it is so kind of you to make us welcome.'

'Call me Big Momma, dear ... Everyone else does. But you Mr Pepper can call me Miss Cherie.'

Big Momma, Cherie Pollitt, offered her arm to Pepper and she and Orlando led the way out through the hallway into a huge drawing room and then out into a large orangery, which had been set with comfortable chairs around a long table. The table was heavily laden with expensive crockery and platters of food. We had obviously arrived just as expected.

'We always eat lunch and breakfast in here,' Big Momma explained. 'Dinner will be in the main dining room.'

We all sat around the table and Orlando held my chair for me as I sat down. He was a perfect gentleman, but I continued to be aware of his peculiar origins. Even though no one around us had given any indication that he was anything other than a normal man.

'You must be all in need of refreshment,' Big Momma continued. When she sat at the head of the table, she lifted a small bell, rang it once and a scurry of servants appeared from behind a screen. I soon realised that the screen hid a door that led into the kitchens.

'Fetch Big Daddy now will you, chile? Tell him our guests are here,' she said to one of the servant girls, who curtsied and hurried away.

Orlando seated himself next to me. Pepper, however, had anticipated this and hurried to the seat on the other side of me before anyone else could occupy it. This was an interesting development, because I had never noticed Pepper behave this way before. Something about Orlando upset him. It was peculiar to have two men vying for my attention like this. It made me feel embarrassed and pleased – even if one of them was just being a protective friend, while the other was a half-demon that under normal circumstances I would have killed on sight.

'Miss Katherine, please let one of the servants take care of that for you,' Big Momma said, observing how I looked around for a place to stow my reticule.

I shook my head. 'That's fine thank you, Big Momma. I always keep this close.'

Big Momma frowned and I saw her exchange a glance with Orlando, as though they already knew why I wouldn't part with my reticule. At that moment a large man, dressed in a white cotton suit, came into the room. 'It's hotter than hell in here,' he said dabbing at his sweaty face with a large handkerchief.

We were introduced quickly to Big Daddy as he took his seat at the far end of the table and I observed him from the opposite side. Big Daddy conformed to his name in many ways. He appeared to be a jovial and benevolent soul, large in height, and happily overweight: he was a man who knew how to appreciate good food and wine. But his size suited him. He sported a well-groomed moustache, white like his thick head of hair, but he also had a pointed white beard that he smoothed down and massaged with his fingers as he spoke.

'Well, it's mighty fine to have you folks here. We will be feasting and partying for the next week. So please do enjoy our hospitality, and ask any of the servants for anything you might want.'

'That's so kind of you, Big Daddy,' Mother said.

We exchanged pleasantries with the family and answered questions about our journey, and our home: all polite enquiries that were designed to put us at our ease.

'Where is Henry?' Mother asked when there was a sufficient lull in the conversation. 'I thought he would have been here to greet us.'

'You know what newly-weds are like,' Big Momma said. 'Henry and Maggie went out earlier for a drive, but just haven't come back yet. I suspect they will be here by this evening for dinner though. Maggie knows we like our formal dinners here, and of course they are expecting you to have arrived.'

I was a little disappointed to find Henry absent when he knew we were coming. I had even expected him to meet us at the station and Mother and Sally were so looking forward to seeing him that the delay felt a little cruel and somewhat thoughtless of him. Of course it had been a long time since I had seen my brother. I had always thought him considerate and caring. Now I was beginning to wonder if I would find him much changed. Of course it was likely that he had just become lost in the happiness of being with his new bride, and who could blame him really?

The servants moved around us in a claustrophobic and confusing bustle as they poured cold wine and fresh water into crystal goblets on the table. Then they filled our plates with cold salmon and crunchy vegetables.

Mother reached over to Sally and, taking the wine goblet out of her hands before she could drain its contents in one go, pushed a glass of water into her fingers instead. Sally sulked after that, but at least she was quiet while we ate the delicious, fresh food.

After the somewhat informal lunch we were shown to our rooms by a silent servant girl. She was around fifteen years old, not as tall as Sally, and she was wearing a black dress with white pinafore over the top. Her skin was paler than the other black servants I had seen, if it hadn't been for the dark, wiry hair peeking out from underneath her hat, I might have taken her for white. Particularly because she also had pale blue eyes.

We walked up the large staircase and were led to the right side of the house, down into a quiet wing. Windows were opened in the rooms as they aired. I surmised that this part of the house had been used very little in recent years.

'Big Momma and Big Daddy's rooms are in the opposite wing. But Misser Henry and Miss Maggie are down there,' said the girl. 'Miss Sally is to have Miss Maggie's old room, and Mrs Lightfoot, you is in the room next door. Miss Katherine you is here ...'

The girl, who we learnt was called Milly, opened up a door and showed me into a beautiful room that was decorated in pastel shades. There was a four-poster double bed in the centre against the far right wall. A row of doors ran along the opposite wall, and Milly pointed out that this was all fitted wardrobe space. The drapes were open, and so were the double doors that lead out onto a wide balcony.

I went outside, only to discover that the balcony passed all the way along the side of house joining up all of the bedrooms.

'This is wonderful,' Mother said coming out onto the balcony, as a male servant came into my room and placed my bags down on the floor.

'I'll unpack for you, Miss Katherine,' said Milly.

'That's all right, I can manage,' I said.

Milly looked at me confused. 'But Big Momma says I'm to be your personal maid while you here, Miss Katherine.'

'But I don't need anyone to ... wait on me ...' I protested.

It was one of those things that the South and the North still disagreed on. But also, I felt to ask Milly to do things for me would make her like a slave again.

'But it's my job to take care of you,' Milly said.

'Let her do it, dear,' Mother said from outside. 'Like she says, it's her *job*.'

Another two maids appeared leading more male servants with Mother's, Sally's and Pepper's bags which were taken to their allocated rooms and I soon realised that everything in the Pollitt Plantation, despite the initial feeling of informality, all had a routine and a rhythm that each of the servants, and the occupants lived by. But I had to remind myself that the servants were employed, and not slaves, which meant then that I could accept Milly's help. Even so, it felt awkward for me. My family had never been excessively wealthy and we had never had slaves or employed servants to do anything for us. We were used to tending to our own needs.

I realised though that I might offend Milly more if I rejected her help and so I allowed her to unpack my clothing trunk.

'I'll take care of this myself,' I said when Milly offered to take my reticule.

Milly nodded and returned to the trunk, pulling out the few dresses I had brought, she hung them up in the wardrobe so that the creases would drop out. When she finished she opened another small door that was hidden behind a dressing screen and showed me a large bath tub.

'Would you like this filling, Miss Katherine?' she asked.

'Now that would be wonderful,' I said. 'But Milly, can you just call me Kat? That's what everyone calls me.'

'Miss Kat, I surely will,' Milly said.

'No ... I meant ... *just* Kat,' I explained.

Milly looked at me confused ... 'Yes, Miss Kat. Whatever you like.'

I realised she didn't understand I was asking her to treat me as an equal but decided to leave it alone. Rome wasn't built in a day, and you couldn't walk into someone else's house and change how they lived either. I decided it was best to go along with the way things were at Pollitt Plantation for now. After all I didn't want the family to think we were criticising the way they lived.

I left Milly to sort out the bath for me and walked down the corridor to see Mother and Sally's rooms. It turned out they were joined by a door between the rooms and so Sally didn't feel too worried about sleeping in this huge house alone.

'If only I had a room like this at home,' Sally said.

She was sitting at an ornate dressing table while Mother unbraided her hair and began to brush it. Another servant girl was unpacking their cases and Mother now had all of her creams, perfume, brushes and combs laid out on top of the dresser.

'I'd have to work very hard indeed to afford something like this ...' I said.

'Or you could just get married ...' Sally said. 'To someone like Orlando ...'

'*Married*?' I laughed. '*Me*?'

I turned away from Sally and Mother hoping to hide the

slight colour that rose again in my cheeks at the mention of Orlando. I explored my feelings. Orlando was nice, but surely I couldn't feel anything like that about him. Especially with his strange demon heritage. such an interest would go completely against the grain.

'Kat, why is that so funny?' asked Mother. 'You'll *have* to do it someday ...'

I shook my head and walked away. I was getting a little tired of Mother assuming I was going to be left on the shelf, because I still wasn't engaged and I was nearly twenty four.

'I had you by the time I was your age,' she had been fond of pointing out recently.

But I didn't agree that I had to get married in order to be happy. In fact most of the marriages I had seen in the last few years appeared to be anything but contented. They all seemed to be about convenience. Or money.

I wasn't the sort of girl who romanticised about love, though it was all fine and nice for others to feel that way. I wasn't romantic at all by nature. Life was too dark, too sinister for me to even consider the possibility of 'settling down' to domesticity. Besides, love wasn't fashionable when it came to commitment. Henry, it seemed, was the exception on that score. Or so his letter had led us to believe.

I went back to my room, and walked out onto the balcony. Milly and a few other servants were still filling the bath for me and I wanted to stay out of their way because the whole 'servant' thing made me feel extremely uncomfortable. Of course, I knew I was an unusual girl for my time, in every way. But generally the society I came from, although service driven, didn't really need people to cook and clean for them. These were things we did for ourselves, and we were proud of it too. The use of servants was only a status symbol in New York. It applied to those with excessive amounts of money, who could afford bigger houses, gas lighting, and their own stables of horses and carriages.

I mulled over our differences as I stood on the balcony overlooking the grounds of the plantation. In the distance I could make out the rows of small houses we had passed on the way in. The servants' homes didn't seem so bad, and they had what appeared to be their own town on the outskirts of the plantation. I tried to accept the environment for what it was. The Pollitts seemed decent people. I didn't think there would be any abuse of their staff, because they were, as Isaac had said, all free. Even so, as I looked over the land I felt that prickle in the back of my head that was a sensation I had often respected and responded to. Something wasn't right here.

I tried to push away the thought as I enjoyed the warm breeze that floated across the balcony. I had no right to make any assumptions about the place or the people. To the casual observer this was a positive and happy household. The only fly in the ointment was Orlando and this was probably enough to set my nerves on edge. Nephilims were rare. They could also be extremely dangerous. Anything connected to the Darkness could not be trusted.

'I don't understand what's wrong?' a female voice said. 'I

thought you loved me.'

'So did I, once …' said a male voice and I realised with surprise that it was my brother Henry who was speaking. 'That was before … Now, I can barely look at you …'

'Henry … why won't you listen? Why won't you let me *explain*?'

'Hush now. We have to play this charade for your family, but that's all I'll do.'

It was later that evening and I slid along the balcony to the room on my right from which the voices issued. The doors were open, and I could hear the sounds of weeping. My heart beat so fast in my chest that I was certain it could be heard. Henry was sitting on a four-poster bed, much like mine, while his wife stood by the door, a silk handkerchief pressed to her eyes as she tried to suppress the quiet sobs that issued from her lips. I had never seen anyone so distraught and I suddenly had to know why.

My mind cast back to the letter we had received from Henry. It told of his elopement with Margaret Pollitt, and of his great love for her. What on Earth had happened in such a short time to change his feelings towards her?

I waited for a while listening to her quiet pleading until I could bear it no longer. The last straw was when Maggie sat beside him on the bed and tried to put her arms around him. Henry pushed her away, though it wasn't rough or cruel, more of a disentangling of himself from her. His face said so much though. There was this strange longing, mingled with disgust as though he was fighting with himself not to give in and hold her.

SAM STONE

I hurried away, back to my own room for fear of being found eavesdropping outside of their door. My heart hurt for Henry, but more for Maggie, who I didn't even know. I'd never seen such a strange expression on Henry's face before. It wasn't like him at all. Something terrible had happened to ruin their happiness, and although I knew it had nothing to do with me, I felt compelled to discover what it was.

5

By the time Milly had finished curling my hair and dressing it in a style more suited to a Southern belle than a native New Yorker, nearly everyone else had gathered for pre-dinner drinks in the expansive drawing room. Bathed and now dressed in one of my new ball gowns – a turquoise blue with black lace trim around the low *décolletage* and short sleeves, especially purchased for the trip to Pollitt Plantation – I followed Milly downstairs.

The drawing room was full of people. I spotted Big Momma and Big Daddy, over in the farthest corner. Big Daddy was deep in conversation with a beautiful young woman with dark auburn hair, who was wearing a deep purple silk dress with ostentatious jewels draped around her neck. I was wearing a simple paste necklace, which made me feel slightly underdressed, despite the expensive dress I was wearing.

Big Momma broke away from the small grouping and hurried to greet me.

'Miss Katherine, don't you just look a picture,' she said. Then she kissed me on both cheeks. 'I know someone who is quite taken with you already.'

She turned me around to face Orlando and I knew that what she said was completely true. Orlando's face lit up when he saw me, and he put down the glass of sherry he was holding and came forward to take my hand. I briefly wondered if he would find me so intriguing if he knew that I regularly killed demons like him.

'Miss Katherine. You are breathtaking,' he said.

'Please, I should have said this before, but can you all just call me Kat? That's what I prefer.'

'Kat?' Orlando said. 'I don't know why, but that does indeed suit you. You are like a cat, with your soft, silent tread. One might even believe you were not of this world.'

I studied Orlando for a moment, wondering if this charming veneer hid the knowledge of who and what I was.

'Who's this then?' said the beautiful brunette appearing at my side. Her expression was serious, and she seemed more than a little put out by Orlando's flowery praise of what he considered to be my virtues.

'I'm Kat,' I said bluntly because I didn't appreciate her scrutiny or the rudeness of her question. 'Who are you?'

'This is my sister,' Orlando explained. 'She can be rather straight speaking sometimes. You'll learn to excuse her, like the rest of us do.'

'Amelia Pollitt-Beaugard,' Big Momma explained. 'Amelia is married to that handsome gentleman right over there. He is Michel Beaugard, of the French Beaugards from Missouri.'

I looked around to see Amelia's husband and discovered that he was indeed a handsome man, though some fifteen years or more older than her. He was sophisticated, with dark hair that was going grey just above his ears and his dark brown eyes, one hidden by a monocle, held a warmth that I did not see in the eyes of his wife. The man came over and politely bowed over my hand and whispered a greeting in a deep French accent. His moustache and pointy beard tickled my hand as he pressed his lips to my fingers.

After the formal introductions, I looked around to see Pepper talking to a frail blonde woman who was wearing a dress that seemed to be far too wide for her slender, delicate frame. Mother and Sally were with Maggie Pollitt.

'Is that Maggie?' I asked Orlando even though I already knew that it was. Orlando took my arm and led me over to meet my new sister-in-law.

Maggie had lovely eyes. Similar in shape to Orlando's but instead of the odd amber that Orlando had, Maggie's were a pale green. She had dark auburn hair, just like Amelia, but she had a prettier face. There was no sign of the woeful tears I had witnessed earlier. I immediately liked her, and felt again an urgent desire to mend whatever rift had begun between her and Henry.

'Your brother will be here soon,' Maggie said. 'He's been having a little trouble with his leg. He gained an injury in the war, and he fell today when we were out. He wrenched it really badly and it hasn't helped his temper. I've heard so much about you though, and I know he's going to be thrilled to see y'all.'

As if on cue, Henry came into the room with a wooden crutch under his left arm.

Mother hurried over to him, but I hung back. Even though we hadn't seen Henry in over five years, he seemed to have changed little in appearance. I wondered about his manner though. Even as he hugged Mother he seemed distant, reserved.

'What happened to your leg?' Mother asked.

'Fell over drunk ... again,' Amelia Pollitt-Beaugard said beside me.

I looked at her sharply, but she didn't have the grace to be embarrassed by her outburst.

'Amelia!' hissed Michel. '*Please.*'

Michel met my eyes and gave me an apologetic look even as Amelia skulked away. She clearly didn't like him correcting her bluntness. I liked her less than I had earlier. She was a strange, unpleasant and somewhat contemptuous character.

When I looked back over at Henry he was hugging Sally. The reunion was touching, but I felt outside of it. You see, I knew that on the inside, Henry had seen things that had changed him during the war, just as I had seen many things during and since. We had both aged, our souls tarnished, and now poor Henry wasn't even obtaining the happiness he truly deserved. I stayed back watching him, almost afraid that he would see the same changes in me that I could detect in him.

Maggie took my arm and pulled me forward as though this gave her the excuse she needed to be near Henry.

'Darlin', your sister is about the loveliest woman I have ever seen,' she said.

Henry looked up at her, his eyes flickered with pain, and then they fell on me and filled with the expression I had hoped to see in his eyes when he looked at Maggie. Love. Happiness. Excitement.

Henry threw his arms around me and hugged me as tightly as he could with one arm. It felt genuine and when I stepped back I saw love and warmth in his eyes, even though I could still detect this innate sadness.

'Kat, I'm so glad you're here.'

After that I made the introduction to Pepper and he and Henry sat down together and discussed the one thing they had in common – the war. Although in the current circumstances it hardly seemed to be the best topic. Even so, the Pollitts didn't seem to mind too much.

'You smelt it didn't you?' Amelia said appearing like a ghost once more beside me.

'What?' I said.

'The fumes from his intoxicated breath …'

I glanced back at Henry. 'He has no more liquor in him than the rest of us do.'

Amelia raised her eyebrows at me. 'Give it time, the night is young.'

At that moment the old black servant we had met at the station, Isaac, came into the drawing room and announced that dinner was served.

When the huge double doors to the dining room were opened, Orlando was at my side offering his arm. I took it without thinking and let him lead me into the room but as I glanced over my shoulder I saw a look of agitation cross the features of my best friend. Though Pepper quickly hid the emotion and offered his arm to the fragile blonde he had been talking to earlier and followed the rest of the group into the room.

The family was spread around a magnificent dining table that seated around forty people. Big Momma and Big Daddy were at either end presiding over the evening like the matriarchs they were.

Place cards indicated where we were to sit and once again I found myself positioned next to Orlando, but on the other side was the charming Michel Beaugard. Opposite me was Pepper with Amelia and the blonde who I learnt was Michel's cousin: her name was Kristina and she was, it appeared, single.

Glancing up the table I noticed that Maggie and Henry had also been separated. Henry was placed between Mother and Big Momma, and Maggie had been positioned all the way down the other side of the table next to Big Daddy. I thought it odd that they had separated the newlyweds like this, but wondered whether it was just the family's attempt at involving everyone at the party.

'Well we are here to celebrate the union of Maggie and Henry,' Big Daddy said.

He stood, holding up his brimming glass of full-bodied red wine.

'I'd like to propose a toast to my eldest daughter and her new husband. I know they are going to be very happy and I look forward to seeing some new grandchildren coming along pretty soon.'

'Not much chance of that …' said Amelia.

Michel frowned at her across the table.

'My other daughter, Amelia, and her husband Michel, have made Big Momma and I so happy and proud with their lovely offspring. Maggie and Henry, I know, will contribute to our ever growing family,' Big Daddy continued. 'To Henry and Maggie.'

We all raised our glasses but the toast felt hollow, insincere, as though Big Daddy knew that things weren't right with Maggie and Henry, and Amelia was the voice of that discontent. His words were like a warning but I didn't know what that warning was.

Even so, Maggie played the happy bride well, and she left Big Daddy's side to walk down to the other end of the table. Then she bent and kissed Henry. He offered her his lips and kissed her back, but as Maggie returned to her chair I noticed how he wiped his mouth on his napkin after the kiss, as though he felt somehow tainted by her touch.

I glanced back at Maggie and saw that Big Daddy had also seen what Henry did. He frowned but said nothing while he took his seat again and the meal commenced.

We had all returned to the drawing room. Some of the ladies were playing cards, while a few of the men had retired to the study for brandy and cigars. Orlando, Pepper and Henry had stayed behind though. It was late and Sally had been taken upstairs to her room by Maggie's former nanny, Nanny Simone, and the girl had gone surprisingly willingly soon after dinner. She was exhausted from the travel and excitement of meeting so many new people, just as Mother, Pepper and I were, but the evening had been fun and I was slowly getting to know more about our new in-laws. Pepper was uncharacteristically quiet, as though he were merely assessing everything, and I noted his measured gaze on Orlando and Amelia many times.

'It's a beautiful night, Miss Kat. May I take you for a walk outside in the gardens?' Orlando said. 'The water fountain looks particularly beautiful by moonlight.'

Orlando's suggestion took a moment to sink in. He was proposing I walk out alone with him. No one had ever done that before and I realised that this situation I found myself in with Orlando was far more alien than the times when I found myself faced by a horde of demons. At least in those circumstances I knew that pulling out a gun was the right response. How do you respond to someone who seems to have a personal interest in you.

'That's not really a good idea,' said Pepper at my side saving me from making the decision. I knew that his words had little to do with the idea of me being alone with a man I barely knew and more to do with the fact that Orlando was a nephilim and couldn't be trusted. Orlando's presence was dulling my senses somewhat, perhaps this was part of the nephilim power?

The bulk of my weaponry was upstairs in my room. It didn't seem appropriate to carry anything down to dinner, although I did have my Perkins-Armley – a discrete purse pistol, made of copper, with a leather handle that made it comfortable in the hand – strapped in a holster around my thigh, hidden under my dress. The gun was made for me some years before by the gunsmith Jerome Perkins. Perkins had been devilled by a rogue demon until Pepper, Martin and I took care of it for him. The gun was his personal thank you to me at the time, but the real payment came when Martin and he exchanged ideas.

'Really, Mr Pepper,' said Orlando. 'Miss Kat will be perfectly safe with me. I have never once in my life taken advantage of a lady.'

Pepper weighed Orlando up carefully. 'It's not *her* safety I'm concerned about.'

'Why don't we *all* go outside?' I suggested.

'What a good idea,' Amelia said. 'May I join you? I could do with some air.'

We walked out through the large veranda doors that led off from the drawing room and out into the expansive gardens. At this side of the house there was a beautiful lawn that panned out towards the cotton plants. The grass was parted with a long path, marked by stone flags that lead down to a large pond, and a small patio which was set with a table and chairs. A row of oil lanterns lit the way down the path, and surrounded the patio area. In the middle of the table was a tray containing a jug of wine and several glasses.

'Looks like we were expected,' said Pepper.

'I had it set a little while again,' said Orlando. 'As I was hoping to take some air.'

Amelia laughed. 'Brother you are so obvious! Just as well you have your chaperone, Mr Pepper, with you, Miss Kat. I've never seen Orlando this smitten before!'

I was glad of the darkness outside which I hoped concealed my awkwardness and embarrassment. I wasn't used to having someone continually thrown at me like this, and the evening had seen quite enough of it. I felt tired, confused by the sense of strangeness in the Pollitt household. There were politics at play which I didn't quite understand yet and I was worried about Henry and Maggie.

'Enough of this silliness,' I said. 'We all know it's just a game you're all playing.'

'Whatever do you mean?' Amelia said.

'I'm rather straight speaking myself, Miss Amelia,' I began. 'And let me tell you …'

A terrified scream echoed from the house cutting short the angry words I was about to use. Words that would have revealed my knowledge about Orlando, and his association with the Darkness.

The scream came again before I realised who it was.

'Sally!' I gasped. I picked up my skirts and ran back towards the house.

6

I took the stairs two at a time, not in the least bit ladylike, with Pepper, Orlando and Amelia close on my heels. As I reached Sally's room, Nanny Simone was just about to enter.

'Miss Sally, whatever is the matter?' the black nanny said as she opened the door.

'Sally?' I rushed in to find her huddled up in the big bed. Her finger was pointing towards the window. The drapes were open, the balcony door ajar.

'Someone came in!' Sally stammered. 'There was a man ...'

'No one here would hurt you, Miss Sally,' soothed Nanny Simone. 'You is safer on Pollitt land than anywhere in the world ...'

I sat on the edge of the bed and hugged her. She sobbed in my arms in a way I had never known her to do.

'He wasn't right ...' said Sally. 'It was something bad, Kat. I know it was. He looked like ... night. I couldn't see his face but …'

'You is just all out of sorts,' Nanny Simone said. 'New place, new people. It's all bound to take a toll on a young girl's mind.'

I looked up to find Henry and Maggie at the door.

'What happened?' asked Henry.

'Nothing but a wandering imagination …' said Nanny Simone.

Maggie's face fell. She glanced around the room. 'Why was she put in *here*?' she demanded. 'All on her own like that?'

'Why Miss Maggie I thought she would like being in your old room. She pretty grown up – too much for the nursery with Miss Amelia's children.'

'I know but …' Maggie stammered. 'But Nanny … not *this* room …'

'Why not this room, Maggie?' I asked.

Maggie shook her head, then she backed away. 'Henry, I'm tired. Let's go to bed now. *Please.*'

Henry frowned, looking around the room with a confused expression on his face. Then he left with Maggie. Pepper, Orlando and Amelia lurked outside, all equally uncertain whether they should enter. A few seconds later Mother appeared at the door and it was soon decided that Sally would sleep in her room from now on.

'We'll move your things next door tomorrow,' said Nanny Simone leading the girl through the partition door into the other room. Soon there was a bustle of servants, setting up a small bed for her.

'Let's all retire for the night. I'm exhausted anyway,' said Mother.

I closed the door between the two rooms, leaving myself inside the room that Sally had previously occupied. Then I waited until everyone else left.

I took stock of the room. Maggie's behaviour had indicated that there was something odd about it. Something so bad, that she had been too afraid to step inside herself. Maybe it was the 'wandering imagination' of the young, as Nanny Simone said. Or maybe it wasn't. I had seen so many things these past few years that I was uncertain whether anything ordinary had ever happened in the world, or whether everything was really down to some supernatural cause.

I was positive that things still hid in the darkness, especially waiting for the vulnerable. Sally was susceptible. Why hadn't I seen that until now? She had been growing up so fast, my world had been so occupied with fending for us, and destroying the evils lurking in our city, that I had barely taken much notice of the changes in her. She was becoming a woman. A dangerous time for any young girl. And here we were in a place that housed a nephilim. Although, whatever had scared Sally, Orlando, at least, wasn't directly involved. He had the best alibi ever – he had been with me. But what other demons might be nearby?

All was silent on the plantation. I went out to the balcony and looked across the lawn and the cotton rows further on. Someone had doused the oil lamps. And I could barely make out anything now.

A breeze moved the plants, or at least I thought it was a breeze. I squinted out over the landscape. Nothing moved. The servants had all retired too it seemed. The house was deathly quiet. And so were the row of servant's homes beyond the cotton fields.

I walked along the balcony towards my room and listened to the sounds of muffled talk coming from Mother's room as I passed. She was still soothing Sally and although I didn't want to make too much of it that night, I was determined to get her to describe exactly what she had seen.

As I reached my open doorway I heard quiet sobs coming once more from Henry and Maggie's room. I felt sick, confused. I didn't want to spy on them but despite myself I moved along closer to the open door of their room.

'Please, Henry. Please …' Maggie pleaded.

'Leave me alone,' Henry said. 'I can't. I just can't do this right now.'

'But you need to let me explain …'

Despite the outward appearance of normality, something was going on in this house. Something to do with Maggie perhaps, and that room …

Along the balcony, just past Maggie and Henry's room I saw another figure. By the shape of the body – the wide ball gown was a dead giveaway – I knew it was female, but the person, seeing my observation, quickly slipped back inside the house before I could reach them.

There was a waft of perfume on the air, one that I recognised as that of Amelia Pollitt-Beaugard. She was curious too, or maybe she knew something already about what was wrong with Henry and Maggie. She had certainly hinted as much throughout the evening. Could it be that Henry really did have a drink problem? I couldn't believe it. All evening he had barely touched his wine, and had refused the offer of brandy in the study. These weren't the actions of a man with a problem.

I passed their room again on the way back to mine. The lamps were off now and all was quiet inside. I felt like a voyeur watching them like this, but I reasoned that my interest was for their own good. Particularly if I could help them in some way.

I returned to the exterior of my own room and went inside. Then I stripped down to my chemise and turned off the oil lamp that was on the dresser. Taking the Perkins-Armley out of the thigh holster, I placed it under my pillow. Then I climbed into the comfortable double bed, rolled over, my hand resting next to the gun, and fell asleep.

A dull, distant, rhythmic beat drifted into my dream like the sound of drums. I woke but the sound faded back into my subconscious as I became more alert. I lay in the dark for a while, listening to the sounds of the house cooling down. The steady creaks and groans that one would expect in a huge structure of this sort. Then I closed my eyes and drifted back to sleep. After that the night was filled with its usual terrors.

7

'It was all just a bad dream,' Mother explained the next morning.

We were alone with Sally in the orangery because no one else had emerged so far. Not even Pepper or Orlando.

'Sally's over-active imagination just got the better of her. Plus she isn't used to being surrounded by so many people. Or the servants. That in itself is enough to give anyone nightmares.'

'I suppose it was brought on by the excitement,' Sally said, trying to think logically and behave like a grown-up. 'And this house is so big. It's kind of scary. But I'm happy to stay in Mother's room from now on. If that's all right with you?'

'Of course, dear,' Mother said. 'They seem to be late sleepers in this household.'

I agreed with her absently, but was grateful for the staff waiting around to serve us breakfast. One of the girls brought in a plate with fried eggs, fresh white bread, some cooked ham and a small plate of cakes, which Sally rapidly tucked into.

Sally consumed a copious amount of freshly squeezed orange juice, cakes and ham as though nothing odd had happened at all the night before and so I began to think that maybe she had imagined it. But the night had been a restless one for me too. Filled with peculiar dreams and floating images.

'I'm so sorry,' Pepper said joining us. 'It's unlike me to sleep in so late.'

'Something in the air. Our hosts haven't emerged yet either,' I said.

I could tell that Pepper hadn't slept too well though. He had dark circles under his eyes.

'Are you all right?' I asked.

'Strange dreams …' he said. 'I didn't sleep as restfully as I would have liked. I thought I heard drums.'

'Really? Me too,' I said looking around to see if we were being observed. 'I need to talk to you … but not here.'

Pepper nodded.

After breakfast I fetched a wide-brimmed hat from my room and Pepper and I went out for a walk. It was hot outside but there was a cool breeze and I knew it would be pleasant to take stock of the land around us.

'I'll meet you outside,' I said to Mother as she took Sally back to their room to supervise the transfer of Sally's things. 'We'll be in the garden somewhere.'

Pepper offered me his arm, which surprised me, but I took it anyway. Then we strolled out through the open drawing room doors onto the large lawn.

'So … what did you dream about?' asked Pepper.

'Demons … the usual,' I shrugged.

'I didn't know you had nightmares.'

'I don't mostly. Just sometimes.'

'You said you heard drums?' Pepper said.

'Yes. The sound woke me up. I thought I'd imagined it until you said you'd heard them too.'

'It's indeed strange.'

'Also, I'm concerned about last night. If Sally says she saw something, then it's likely she did.'

'But she's just said it was a dream.'

'I think we can probably rule that out. Although, I did briefly consider it was the truth. Something isn't right here. We've been around this stuff long enough to know when something is wrong, haven't we? I can sense it. It's like …'

'What …?'

I shrugged, finding the sensation difficult to explain. But the uneasiness continued that morning, a feeling of unreality surrounded Pollitt Plantation and it was like nothing I had experienced before. As though by being on their land we had been surrounded by some form of cocoon that separated us from the outside world.

'I don't know,' I said finally. 'Perhaps I'm just so used to being a city girl. This place feels …'

'Like we're in the middle of a void?' Pepper finished.

'Yes.'

'Maybe we should speak to some of the house servants.

Ask them if they've seen anything strange? Particularly this dark figure that Sally saw.'

'Good plan. Pepper?'

'Yes, Kat?'

'I *know* there's something very wrong here. I can't define it. It's just a feeling I have.'

'I have the same feeling,' Pepper said. 'There's Orlando, of course ...'

'Yes. But he seems ... benign. I don't think he even knows what he is.'

'Is that possible?'

'The neph we killed back home said a lot of them didn't know what they were. At the time I was thinking he was just trying to save his own neck. Now, I'm not so sure. It seems unlikely that Orlando knows anything. Isn't it possible that if something is half-demon and half-human that the human side could be dominant, not the demon side?'

'I suppose so. But we know that most things demon related are usually drawn to the Darkness. But what about Big Momma? Does she know that a demon seduced her? Or was she somehow tricked into thinking Big Daddy was Orlando's father.'

I was quiet for a moment. 'She's very flirtatious. Perhaps ... Do you think perhaps she had an affair, but didn't know the man was a demon?'

'It would explain why Dig Daddy barely acknowledges Orlando is in the room,' Pepper said.

'You noticed that too, huh?'

'Why good morning,' called a voice across the lawn.

Pepper and I turned to find Orlando strolling towards us as though he knew we were talking about him.

'Good morning,' Pepper said solemnly.

I let Orlando take my hand and watched him bow over my fingers. He was a picture of formality, yet his home was filled with secrets and inconsistencies.

'You're going riding?' I observed, his clothing was a cross between cowboy and plantation owner. A mix of formal and informal.

'Just returned. I'm something of an early riser. I like to ride in the morning. It helps clear my head for the day. I hope you slept well.' Orlando glanced back at the house. 'I don't always sleep too well when I first arrive here ... All the excitement I guess. It will be better this evening though I'm sure. And now I had better change for the day. I know Big Momma has some kind of garden party planned, with a few of the local plantation owners coming to call. Miss Kat, Mr Pepper ...'

Orlando tapped his wide-brimmed hat and bowed his head but as he turned I caught hold of his arm.

'Why didn't you sleep well?' I asked.

Orlando's expression told me he was a little taken aback by my bluntness.

'It's probably just the heat ...' he said but somehow I didn't believe him. 'But ...'

'Yes?'

'Nothing ...'

'Was it the drums?' I said.

Orlando shrugged and as my hand slipped away from his arm he bowed his head and walked away.

The day passed quickly and aside from the pleasant garden party, uneventfully, but as evening approached a strange disquiet descended on the house. I returned to my room to change for the evening and as I approached, found my door open. I could hear Milly and one of the other servant girls talking as they were preparing my bath. They were unaware that I entered as they sloshed hot buckets of water into the tub.

'He's mighty disturbed,' said Milly. 'Can't you feel it?'

'Hush up, now. You might bring that old thing in here to listen in,' said the other girl.

'Now Celia. You know Simone say that he only interested in the doings of white folks …'

'I don't care what he interested in. I done seen more of that ghost since the girl arrived … he attracted to 'em as they growing …' Celia said.

I slid closer to the door, hoping to hear more. I could see the girls through the crack in the door now. Milly was facing the door, Celia was leaning over the bath.

'It be fine, she safe now she in with her Momma …' Milly said. Then her eyes flickered towards the door. 'Why, Miss Kat, you back here and just in time for your bath.'

I saw a small guilt blush colour Milly's cheeks as she noticed me. Celia scurried out of the room and quickly away.

'Thank you, Milly. I'm so ready for some time alone,' I said.

I let her help me out of the cotton dress I'd been wearing for most of the day.

'I hung out the dress you indicated this morning,' Milly said pointing to a beautiful lilac gown that hung over the door of the wardrobe. 'It's real pretty.'

I went into the bathroom, removed my chemise and slipped into the water. It was the perfect temperature for a hot night, warm but not too much, and I listened to Milly bustling around the room preparing everything to help me dress again.

As I washed away the perspiration of the day, things suddenly went quiet in the room next door.

'Milly?' I asked. 'Are you all right in there?'

When she didn't answer I assumed that she had merely left the room for a while to fetch something. Still feeling shy about being naked around her, I climbed out of the bath and picked up the large towel that she had left folded on the small bureau in the room. I wrapped it around myself. The towel was big enough to cover me twice. It felt warm and soft.

I walked back into the bedroom. The door to the corridor was closed, though the balcony doors were open slightly to let in the cool night air. I rubbed myself dry, then reached for my clean chemise, dropping it over my head in one practiced move. As I began to button the front of the under-dress I became aware of the lack of light in the room. Goosebumps broke out over my arms. The hair stood up on the nape of my neck.

On instinct I looked around for my bag of weapons, then remembered I had stowed them in the bottom of the wardrobe.

KAT ON A HOT TIN AIRSHIP

I hurried towards the cupboard, then saw a blur of movement out of the corner of my eye. I turned to look directly at the door. A black void spread across the room, blocking my view of the door. I opened the wardrobe without taking my eyes away from the shadow, and felt inside for my carpet bag. What manner of demon was this that could dampen the light from one corner of the room to the other? It was as though it covered it, or maybe the light shunned it. I wasn't sure which. My hand fell on the bag and I pulled it out, never taking my eyes away from the shadow.

Still keeping my eyes on the blur, I reached inside the bag. I felt around among my weapons. My fingers caressed the clockwork operated cross-bow, the semi-automatic laser pistol, and more importantly the back-pack tank that held over a hundred small bullets that I could load into the reconditioned Remington 1958, which was a beautiful, brutal and efficient automatically loading gun, designed by Martin when we were trapped in Tiffany's jewellery store fending off a horde of zombies. The bullets contained diamond shards – the hardest substance you can imagine – and when fired from the weapon they tore up anything in its path. I passed over the gun though. I knew this weapon would be useless against a being that failed to have substance. My fingers scrambled around and fell on my boot knife. A silver blade, tempered with diamonds. Probably worth more than a lot of the obscene jewellery that the Pollitt women seemed to favour. And maybe it could be a deterrent. Silver, Pepper, Martin and I had observed, was repellent to most demonic creatures. We didn't know why … it just was – and as for diamonds. They didn't seem to like those that much either.

I pulled out the knife.

'Show yourself, freak,' I said holding the blade before me.

The blur moved again. It shifted away from the door and at that moment, Milly chose to return to the room.

Milly came to a halt on the threshold. She wrapped her arms around herself, shivering as though an intense cold wind had just blown over her. Her eyes shifted around the room, showing far more white than I would have thought possible as they widened and came to rest on the blur. *She could see it too*! She gasped, then clapped her hands across her mouth as though she were afraid to make a sound that might draw attention to herself as she backed away.

The blur spread over the back of the room, slid across the bed, and rushed towards the balcony.

I tracked it, knife in hand, until it disappeared out into the night. I hurried towards the doors and looked outside. Nothing stirred. The lawn was lit up for the evening, and I could see a row of carriages driving towards the house.

'It's gone,' I called to Milly.

She peered in through the door at me. Wide-eyed, afraid.

'Get in here,' I ordered.

The girl rushed to obey. Coming inside the room warily, before closing the door behind her.

I indicated the edge of the bed. 'Sit down.'

Milly stared at the knife in my hand. Suddenly her fear

switched from the shadow and became focused on the blade and on me. I reached into the carpet bag and pulled out the sheath. I slid the knife in, and placed it back into the bag.

'What was *that*?' I said nodding my head towards the balcony.

'I don't know ...' she stammered.

'You and Celia were talking about it ...' I prompted.

'Oh lordy!' Milly said, and then she dissolved into sobs. 'I can't. I can't talk about ... it ... him ...'

'Milly, do I look like an ordinary woman to you?'

'Why ... yes ... of course ...'

'Do ordinary women carry weapons?'

Milly glanced at the carpet bag then back at me. 'Weapons, Miss?'

'I'm a demon slayer, Milly. And you need to tell me everything you know about that thing we both just saw ... Because ... I'm probably the only person around here that can help you get rid of it for good.'

Milly shook her head, 'I didn't see nothin' Miss Kat, only you, pointing that knife at me. I didn't see nothin' ...'

8

'It's so wonderful having you all here,' Maggie said taking my hand. 'I was thinking that you might help me persuade Henry to let us come and visit you in New York. I've never been there, and I think it will do us some good.'

'Mother and I would love that,' I said.

Isaac appeared with a silver tray and offered us a glass of something long and cloudy.

'What is this?' I asked.

'It's lemonade with gin,' Maggie explained. 'Isaac, I hope you prepared a non-alcoholic glass for Miss Sally?'

Isaac nodded. 'Of course, Miss Maggie.'

At that moment a gaggle of small boys ran into the room. I soon learnt that these were Amelia and Michel's children. The grandchildren that Big Daddy had spoken of the evening before. We hadn't seen them all day or the evening before and so their presence surprised me.

Maggie frowned when she saw them. 'Nanny Simone keeps them out of everyone's way most of the time. They are … a little spoilt and badly behaved.'

'We came to sing a goodnight song to Big Daddy,' one of the obnoxious boys said, while another one picked his nose and smeared the contents he extracted over the arm of his younger brother.

The boys sang their song, which was hopelessly out of tune, then they played noisily in the corner of the room. Big Momma patted and petted them until eventually Nanny Simone came to take them all away again. I caught the eye of Amelia as she watched her boys taken by the nanny. She was smiling proudly, but there was something else in her expression that told me she was also deliberately flaunting the children in front of Maggie.

'It will be your turn soon enough,' said Big Momma sliding up to Maggie. 'Maybe you'll give us a girl. A nice granddaughter that I can spoil with beautiful things. Boys are wonderful, but they tend to be so mischievous. Why look at how adorable Miss Sally is? She's all grown-up and ladylike. Yes, Maggie. I would really like you to have a daughter soon.'

'Well I won't have much say on that, Momma,' Maggie said. She laughed but the sound was flat and it seemed to be a real effort for her to sustain.

Big Momma was called away to some other distant cousin who had joined us that night.

'Not much chance of that though, hey Maggie?' said Amelia.

Her smile was cruel. I was positive that it was her I had seen outside Henry and Maggie's room the night before. Why she was there I could only guess, but I liked her less every day.

'You know Big Daddy wants an heir from you, *Cherie*,' Amelia continued.

'Well Maggie and Henry are newlyweds. What's the rush? There's plenty of time yet,' I said.

Amelia and Maggie exchanged glances. There was a subtext that I didn't understand and had no right to interfere with.

'I don't care about inheriting the plantation,' Maggie said suddenly.

'That's just as well,' said Amelia. 'With the husband you picked ...'

Amelia walked off and I stared after her as I realised that this growing antagonism between them might be about money, rather than just sibling rivalry.

'What is it with her?' I asked.

Maggie turned away and said nothing, but I followed her gaze and saw that she was staring across the room at Big Daddy. She seemed lost and I wished that I knew her enough to actually become a *confidante*. If I knew what the problem was, maybe I could help.

'Maggie, I want you to know you can ... tell me anything ...'

Maggie's eyes were sad, but she forced a smile on her face. 'Whatever are you talking about? Pay no mind to Amelia. She always taunts me. Some folks around here resent anyone from the North. They blame their own misfortunes on them. But the truth is Amelia and Michel ... they should have reformed their land like Big Daddy did. They would still have all the money and privilege they once had.'

'You're saying that Amelia and Michel are ... not as wealthy as they appear?'

'Kat, they have been foolish, and Michel ... he's not too good with money and cards ... But I don't like to gossip. But I just wanted to ...'

'Reassure me that nothing was wrong with you and Henry?'

Maggie blushed. 'Why ever would you think there was?'

I hugged her, saw the tears that threatened to spill from her eyes and quickly changed the subject. Now was not the time, but Maggie clearly needed a friend.

'Kat?' Pepper said interrupting us. 'Would you care to take an evening stroll with me?'

I was a little surprised that Pepper had even asked, but as I met his eyes I knew he had something to tell me that he didn't want anyone else to hear.

'Dinner won't be long,' Maggie said. 'In fact, I need to go and find Henry. He hasn't come down yet.'

Once outside I told Pepper about my sighting of the shadow, or ghost, or whatever it was and about the conversation I had heard Milly and Celia have.

'And she wouldn't tell you anything at all?' Pepper said.

'No. How did you get on?'

'I spoke to Isaac. But he laughed off what I said. Told me that was "superstitious nonsense, and not usually the kind that white folks indulged in". But I felt he knew something.'

I glanced back at the house. 'Pepper, there's something wrong with Henry and Maggie too.'

Even though I didn't want to let out my brother's secrets I found myself revealing what I had overheard on the balcony.

'They are really unhappy and I don't know why. Amelia is part of this too. She keeps hinting that my brother drinks … but he's barely touched a drop in the last few days: I've been watching him. Then tonight she implied they would never have children.'

'If there's a rift between them … that may be the case,' Pepper said.

'But why? They are married and … oh. I see what you mean, they may not be consummating …'

I drew in the evening air and tried not to remember that I was having a very intimate conversation with a man. Pepper was after all my best friend, and he didn't count in that way at all, I told myself. After all we had seen and been through, this was nothing.

'I wish I could just ask them outright. Why does everything have to be so … *proper*?

'It seems to me that a lot of this is about Maggie,' Pepper said.

'How do you surmise that?'

'Well, Maggie ran away with your brother. To do that they must have been very in love.'

'Precisely ... so what has happened since?'

'They came back here ...'

We both looked back at the huge white house. The windows looked like eyes watching us. And I sensed that ripple of adrenaline that usually accompanied some kind of demon visitation.

Henry was on the balcony smoking a cigar. He appeared to be looking out over the cotton plants, and towards the servants' quarters. We saw Maggie come out to him. She seemed awkward and unnatural as she approached. Not at all like the happy newlywed she should be. She reached out a hand and placed it on his arm, but Henry pulled away as though her touch burned him.

'You see?' said Pepper.

'Yes ... they definitely have some disagreement ...'

'I don't mean them. Look behind Maggie ...'

The balcony was only lit by the light coming from their room and so it was difficult to make out anything more than their shapes. But as I squinted upwards I noticed the dark shadow that lurked behind Maggie, a shadow that couldn't possibly be there given the light and the way it reflected outwards. Indeed the natural shadow from both of them fell over the edge of the balcony, confirming that the dark shape we could see wasn't part of Maggie at all. But as she moved it followed, as though it were inexplicably attached to her.

'It's up there with them,' I said.

Henry left Maggie and went back inside. She watched him go, then turned and threw an irritated glance in the direction of the shadow.

'Leave me alone, damn you!' she said.

I had withdrawn my Perkins-Armley from the thigh holster under my dress and was pointing it towards the shadow as I ran across the lawn towards the house. Pepper was at my side, sword drawn from his cane. There was an exterior staircase that led upstairs, and the two of us hurried up there and onto the balcony towards Maggie and Henry's room, but by the time we got their the shadow was gone and so was Maggie.

'What the hell is it?' I said. I was beginning to feel really frustrated by the whole situation.

'It did looked like, a ghost, a phantom of some sort ...' Pepper said. 'Just as you described.'

'Well it's obviously causing this family some problems. So, how do we kill it? Or exorcise it I suppose would be the right term ...'

'I don't know, Kat. I really don't. This isn't like anything we've come across before.'

9

The drums entered my dreams again, building to a barbaric crescendo that culminated in what sounded like a scream of abject terror.

'Sally!'

I leapt from my bed, gun in hand – extracted from beneath my pillow by pure instinct – and hurried to the door that led out into the corridor. This was the direction the noise came from, and now, wide awake I could still hear the drums beating in the distance. I hadn't imagined them at all!

I threw open the door and stared down the dark corridor. All was silent. It was as though the scream had fallen on deaf ears, or only I had heard it.

I waited. The landing remained empty. No one was coming, and so, thinking myself a victim of that overactive imagination that Nanny Simone spoke of, I went to close the door with the intention of returning to my bed.

Could it be that I had been dreaming after all?

The drums abruptly stopped.

A low sob permeated the walls as though the house was crying. I froze.

The sound came again. Small, frightened. Perhaps the tears of a child. It wasn't Sally though, I was sure of that much.

I considered fetching the small lamp on the table, but I have excellent night vision. A lamp would spoil that, and would mean that my hand was not free to fend off any potential attacker.

I reached for my robe, slipped it over the thin cotton nightshift I was wearing and picked up my Perkins-Armley. The leather handle felt warm in my palm as I pulled back the safety catch.

I closed the door behind me and crept along the corridor towards where I thought the sound was. As I passed Mother's room, I pressed my ear to the door and listened. From within I could hear the whistle of Mother's breathing, but otherwise all was quiet. Reassured that the scream had not come from Sally, I moved on.

I passed the room that Sally had initially occupied and then went on towards Pepper's room. I listened at his door. I was surprised that he hadn't come out by now. He usually had a sixth sense about these things. I contemplated knocking and waking him, but I was still uncertain if this was all my imagination – Pepper's silence seemed to confirm that there had been no loud scream – and I didn't want to appear to be an hysterical female. Not that I really believed Pepper would think that of me. But it did briefly cross my mind.

I had noticed that there was something about this house that was changing us all, making us behave differently. And I have to confess, I was feeling nervous, far more so than normal. Part of it was because I wasn't sure what I was dealing with. Lack of knowledge of the creature also meant that I didn't know how to destroy it. This made me feel slightly insecure. I mean, how do you kill something that appears to be nothing more than shadow and has no corporeal form?

Beyond Pepper's room were several other doors, which I assumed all led onto other bedrooms. I listened at them all, hearing nothing. I couldn't remember if any of the other visiting family were down here, but I had a feeling that all of these rooms were empty.

I was about to turn back when I heard the whimper again. It appeared to be coming from the very last room. I reached for the handle and turned it, but the door was locked.

I had left my lock picks back in my room. I glanced at the gun in my hand – this was no use in this situation, though it may well be handy at some point. I felt that surge of frustration and anger again. An irrational mood crashed over me. I wanted to see inside the room and find out who was crying, and more importantly why. The thought that I couldn't get inside made me feel an overwhelming rage.

I took a deep breath. What was wrong with me? I was usually so calm and methodical in these situations. I turned to leave and at that moment the door clicked open, as though someone on the other side had turned the lock.

The door swung inwards of its own volition and light filtered out from an oil lamp that was lit inside the room. I stepped forward cautiously. I saw a little boy sitting in the middle of an overlarge bed in the centre of the room. He was crying softly.

I lowered my gun and crossed the threshold.

There was a rush of air, it felt as though I had just walked under a waterfall, and the room beyond was a vacuum of sound. I could now hear nothing of the normal house creaks and groans beyond and the little boy in the bed rubbed his eyes and mewed softly as though he were afraid. I hid the gun at my side so that I wouldn't frighten him further.

'Are you all right?' I asked. 'Did you have a bad dream?'

The boy looked up at me. He appeared afraid for a moment.

'What's your name?' I said.

The boy just stared at me. The light was caught in his eyes, making them appear abnormal. They glowed as though gold shards reflected in them.

'I guess you must be one of Amelia's little boys?' I said.

'How did you get in here?' asked the boy.

'I came through the door,' I said.

'It was locked. I'm not allowed out.'

'Why not?' I asked approaching the bed.

'I was bad. I'm being punished.'

'Getting into mischief is part of growing up,' I said. It all now made perfect sense. 'So what did you do? Parents have a habit of overreacting to ...'

I stopped talking and stared into his eyes. Now I was closer I could see them more clearly. The child had amber eyes, just like Orlando's. He was a nephilim.

'Perhaps I can talk to your mother. Ask her to forgive you,' I mumbled trying to hide the recognition.

If this boy was Amelia's it meant that she too had been seduced by a demon. Her child was half-demon, just like her brother was. The connotation was not lost on me. It also meant that there was a demon living on Pollitt Plantation. Maybe it was the ghost I had seen, or maybe that was just drawn here by the evil it felt.

'What was it she was punishing you for?' I asked again.

The little boy smiled. 'I tried to drown my sister.'

'You did *what*?'

'It was only a game …' said the boy. 'She can be so irritating.'

The boy was smiling widely now. As though he had just told me the nicest thing in the world. I found myself backing away to the door. The boy was clearly insane, or just plain evil. I remembered the weapon in my hand and tried to raise my hand, but it felt too heavy, as though some cord had tied it to my side. I looked down. I felt terror. Fear like I had never known. This thing was controlling my arm. I couldn't raise it no matter how hard I tried. I had to get out of here. Call for help.

My other hand fumbled at the door, twisting the handle. I didn't even remember it closing behind me.

'It's locked,' said the boy. 'I told you.'

'No … I just walked through it!'

'No. That would have been impossible.'

My limbs became weak. Arms and legs began to ache with the effort of forcing them to move backwards against the door.

The boy remained in the bed, staring at me.

'You're not really here,' he said as though he were trying to help me, but I knew that couldn't be the case. He was evil, through and through. Not at all like Orlando … I was starting to believe I had been right that nephs could choose the human or the demon path. Perhaps choice was the key.

'You don't have to be this way …' I said. 'You can deny the demon side in you.'

The boy threw back the covers and slipped to the edge of the bed. He was looking at me with intense curiosity.

He slid bare-footed onto the cold floor. He was wearing a long white nightshirt that almost reached his ankles and hung from his shoulders as though it were several sizes too big.

'Who are you?' he asked. 'Why are you here?'

He began to walk towards me. I felt weak, defenceless and terrified. All emotions I was unaccustomed to feeling. The weight of his gaze drained all the energy from me and I fell back against the door as my knees gave.

I found myself tumbling back into the corridor as though the door I had been struggling to open had never even been there.

I stared through the doorway. The boy stood wide-eyed, unafraid, but curiosity was still the main focus of his expression.

Now I had crossed back into the house a rush of sound

came back to my ears. The creaks of settlement, the subtle sounds of snoring from a room somewhere along the corridor. I felt the strength returning to my fingers and although I was tangled up in the hem of my robe I pulled my gun in front of me and aimed it at the half-breed demon as he stood in the doorway.

He didn't step closer however. As he reached towards the frame, a surge of energy, like a rush of wind, pushed him backwards. He stumbled, fell and turned to stare back at me as the door slammed shut.

I heard a loud click. A lock firmly engaged. Then I stumbled to my feet and hurried back down the corridor.

'There's nothing there,' whispered Pepper.

'This is impossible,' I said quietly. 'Pepper there was a door here. I opened it. I went inside. There was a nephilim child inside.'

Pepper examined the wall. It was smooth, covered with patterned paper that would have shown the crack if a secret door had been there. The skirting boards were all one perfect piece along to the next room.

'Do you think I *imagined* it?' I asked, as Pepper's thorough examination revealed that a door could not possibly have been hidden in those few short moments when I had gone to his room.

Pepper stepped back and frowned. 'No. I don't. But *possibly* you were dreaming. However I'm inclined to think you saw what you say you saw.'

'Thank you,' I was relieved that my friend believed me,

even if the evidence wasn't there to support what I had seen.

'I just don't know how this is possible though,' Pepper said. 'But then, nephilim's are still unknown to us. We have no idea what magic they are capable of performing. The best thing we can do is check this out again in the morning.'

'You're right.' I'd had quite enough excitement for one night.

We turned back quietly down the corridor with the intention of returning to our rooms.

'Whatever the power is, I don't think – despite his comment about trying to drown his sister – that the child was doing it,' I whispered suddenly. 'It was almost like I was expelled from the room, and when he tried to follow me out, he was thrown back inside. That's when the door closed and locked again.'

I stopped outside Pepper's room and turned again to say goodnight.

'I'll walk you back to your room,' Pepper said.

'No need. I'm only three doors away.'

'I know but this place has me rattled. I'll feel happier if ...'

'All right,' I said. I was badly shaken by the experience, particularly the way my strength had been taken from me.

I opened my bedroom door as soon as we reached it and Pepper went inside, lit the lamp and looked around the room. I waited patiently, allowing him this little piece of male pride. Even though I felt there was no need, it did give me some reassurance.

'All clear,' he said after checking inside the wardrobe for the third time.

'Thank you,' I said. Then I leaned over and gave him a kiss on the cheek. 'I'm feeling exhausted now.'

Pepper backed out of the room, but his hand had gone to his cheek where I had kissed him. As though the gesture had come as a complete shock. And, I must admit, it surprised me too. I don't know why I had done it. Kissing Pepper, even on the cheek, was something I had never even considered doing before. I closed the door quickly, and left my stunned friend on the other side. Was I turning into some kind of weak and sentimental female after all? This house, this place, was definitely making me behave more out of character every day.

For good measure I went to my carpet bag and pulled free the Remington-Crewe laser. I hadn't used this weapon for a while: the last time was in the warehouse when Pepper and I finished off the skinners. This weapon always felt good in my hand. I had seen it slice through metal, it could cut down anything corporeal that the Darkness had to offer.

I turned off the lamp, and climbed back into the bed again. My behaviour was odd. I knew that. All of us were acting strangely. Even Pepper with this new found gentlemanly concern for me, especially when he knew I was completely capable of taking care of myself.

I slid the Remington-Crewe under my pillow beside the Perkins-Armley after making sure the safety was on. Then I turned over and closed my eyes.

As I drifted off to sleep, I felt strangely cold. As though there was a cool breeze blowing in from the balcony. But I remembered that I had closed the doors earlier. Although I remained still my eyes opened. I forced my breath to regulate, mimicking the sleep-breathing that I had heard coming from Mother's room earlier.

The cold grew more intense. Through slitted eyes I could see my expelled breath clouding the air. Carefully I slipped my hand under the pillow and felt the cold copper of the gun against my fingers as I wrapped them around the handle.

There was something in the room with me. I felt it move, a kind of disruption in the atmosphere, as well as the change in temperature that signified, and confirmed, its presence and I knew it was the shadow from earlier.

I secured the Remington-Crewe in my palm as quietly as I could, then I felt a stifling, claustrophobic sensation as the shadow drew closer to the side of my bed. A heavy pressure rested on top of the bedclothes. If the thing had weight, then it had substance. I drew the gun, pulled back the covers and fired the laser directly into the space the thing occupied. Light exploded into the room, but inky-blackness was all I could see above me.

The weight increased and I found myself crushed down. I tried to yell, but the thing covered my face. My breath was stifled. I struggled. The Remington-Crewe fell from my fingers and my hands clawed at thin air. A thick substance appeared under my finger nails and smeared my skin wherever I made contact with the space the creature should have occupied. It was there, but it wasn't, and it was somehow killing me.

The door burst open and the thing released me. I saw Pepper illuminated like an avenging angel, sword spinning in the air, as I slowly lost consciousness.

10

'How are you feeling?' asked Mother as I opened my eyes.

It was morning and the light streamed in through the open curtains, even as fresh air wafted through the open balcony doors.

'What happened?' I said. I tried to sit but my head hurt. It was as if I had drunk too much of the fine wines and champagnes on offer the previous night, even though I knew that I barely touched a drop.

'That was what I was about to ask you,' said Mother. 'You fired a gun in the middle of the night. Mr Pepper was the first to arrive to see what happened, I came next. In fact the whole household was awakened by it.

'Oh goodness! Mother, I'm sorry. There was someone in here. Someone attacked me.'

'There was no one in here. The balcony doors were shut, and we were in the corridor. There was no way this attacker could escape.'

The bedroom door opened and Henry came in. Since we had arrived in New Orleans I had barely seen him and we hadn't spent any time alone at all.

'Could I ... speak to Henry alone please, Mother?' I asked.

Mother sighed. 'I've been here with you all night. I was quite worried my dear.'

'I'm sorry. I didn't mean to cause you any worry at all.'

'Well. I suppose I should go and change for the day anyway,' Mother said.

Henry closed the door after her and hobbled over with his crutch, taking a seat beside the bed.

'Sorry Kat,' he said.

'What for?' I pulled myself up into a sitting position.

'I invited you here and it hasn't exactly been pleasant.'

'Our hosts are very amiable,' I pointed out. 'But Henry what is going on? You and Maggie ... your relationship isn't what I thought it would be.'

'It's a long story.'

'Well I'm not going anywhere at the moment.'

'I don't know where to start,' he said.

'Try the beginning. That usually works for most people.'

Henry nodded but he took a moment to gather his thoughts before he began his story.

'I was off duty, wanting to wind down after a hard day of negotiations. You see my Major appointed me to the diplomatic posse who were trying to smooth things out in New Orleans. Our job was to help rebuild relationships between the

North and South. And we had to work particularly with the landowners. They had lost out the most in the war and were trying to find new ways to live, particularly working alongside blacks and not treating them badly, or like slaves anymore.

'So, I was kicking back in this bar. The truth was I losing badly in a game of poker and then this Southern gentleman came and sat down beside me. I only glanced at him while I continued to play, but I noted his expensive clothing and wondered briefly what he was doing in this cheap bar downtown. Though I didn't wonder for long.

'It was as though his presence brought with it lady luck. My fortunes turned. I began winning and winning well. Better than I had ever done. After a while all of the players dropped out. They couldn't sustain the level of loss I suppose. But by then I was happy and ready to quit and taking my winnings on back to my hotel.

'When the game was over, the Southern gentleman invited me to have a drink with him at the bar. I was curious about him and so agreed. It wasn't lost on me that his sudden appearance had changed my luck and I didn't mind buying him a drink based on that. I was feeling relaxed and happy. It made me unusually gregarious, and the man was easy company.

'As we sat down, the bartender came over and took our orders. The man ordered sour mash whiskey and I went along with it. He introduced himself as the bartender poured our drinks and for the first time I looked directly at him. That's when I noticed his strange coloured eyes. It was also the first time I met Orlando Pollitt.

'Orlando and I became friends. When I learnt he was Big Daddy Pollitt's son I couldn't believe my luck. I'd been trying to get Big Daddy involved in the negotiations but every time one of our messengers invited him he declined to come.

'When Orlando invited me over to the Plantation for dinner, I realised things were looking up. He told me he had already known who I was before I sat down, and he wanted his father to become involved in the discussions. Orlando thought it was important to the future of the South.

'The Plantation wasn't what I expected though. You know that Big Daddy had already reformed his way of working long before the war, and so Pollitt Plantation was the only thriving one in the area. I realised immediately that this was why Big Daddy had refused my invitations. He didn't need us. He was doing fine all on his own. But this also meant that we needed him. A great deal. His insight would be a positive example to all of the other landowners.

'That evening though, the first time here, I saw Maggie and I was immediately attracted to her. She was like honey to a bee for me. A fact that Orlando encouraged with open generosity. It was he that made it possible for Maggie and I to meet and be alone, and finally to fall so in love that we just had to be together.

'Of course when Big Daddy found out, he got into a rage. He was calling Orlando all the names of the devil and I was banned from ever stepping foot on Pollitt land again. This meant that all the good work I had been doing with him to help at the next conference just all crumpled. I didn't care though. I resigned my commission – even though the Colonel tried to talk me out of it. And Orlando helped Maggie and I elope. "It's the least I can do," he said.

'So, Maggie and I ran away together.'

Henry paused and his eyes glistened with unshed tears of his remembered happiness.

'That was the happiest day in my life, Kat. When Maggie said "I do". I've never felt such joy.

'Of course, Big Daddy finally came around to accepting the situation. I think Orlando, bless his kind soul, had much to do with it. He loved Maggie and wanted her to be happy. And she was. We were. Until now.'

'What's changed?' I asked.

Henry sighed. He bowed his head a moment as though he had to take time to get round to the awful thing that had ruined his life.

'All was good. We bought our own place. It wasn't all of … this …' he said gesturing around himself to indicate the wealth and ostentation on the plantation. 'But it was good. The trouble was, Big Daddy wanted his eldest daughter to have the best of everything.

'So, when we all began to make nice. He asked us to move back onto Pollitt land.'

Henry grew quiet again.

'I was all for it. But both Maggie and Orlando said it might not be such a good idea. I didn't understand. Not then.'

I sat up in the bed, making myself a little more

comfortable as Henry continued. I felt as though I was on the cusp of some revelation. That somehow I was going to learn exactly what had happened here, and what the dark shadow was that haunted the house.

'I agreed to come and visit the Plantation with Maggie, see how we got on here. But we decided we would still maintain our own little house in New Orleans. The night before we came over though, something really peculiar happened.

'I had been called to see the Colonel, he wanted to persuade me to take my job back. He said I was a "fine officer and a great negotiator" and that my marriage to Maggie might actually help things in the long run in the area. I told him I would consider it. I wanted to talk to Maggie about his offer and so I came straight back to our little house.

'The house was in darkness as I arrived home. It was late and so I thought Maggie had gone to bed. I went into our parlour, poured myself a brandy to help me relax a little while I thought over the Colonel's words.

'A little while later I woke to find I had fallen asleep in the chair by the fire. I stood up, stretched a little then went upstairs to bed.

'As I opened the bedroom door, I found Maggie lying on top of the bed. Her clothing was all in a disarray and she was breathing really hard as though she had caught some kind of fever. The room was cold. I pulled the blanket up over her and then turned to the window, planning to shut the door that was open, which I thought was the cause of the chill in the room. Out of the corner of my eye I saw a man leaving through the door. I was so shocked I almost didn't know what to do. Then this rage came over me.

'I pulled out the hand pistol I keep in the drawer beside the bed and I rushed at the door, calling and yelling after the blaggard. By the time I reached it, the man was gone. I returned to the bed, shook Maggie awake and asked her what had happened. She denied that anyone had been there.

'Well I love my wife, and so I wanted to trust her. I could put it down to tiredness, me half asleep like that stumbling into our room, but the whole scenario worried at my mind. I was sure there was something Maggie wasn't telling me. So we carried on as normal. The next day she was fine and lovely, and full of love for me as we packed up the carriage and drove into the Plantation.

'When we got here Maggie began to behave oddly. During the day she was fine, but in the evening she would get all nervous and edgy. Sometimes she would start to cry and beg me to leave this place with her. She said that if we didn't leave soon something awful was going to happen. Of course I didn't believe her. I thought that her problem was just she didn't like being here anymore. Not with Big Daddy the way he was behaving. "He's trying to buy you," she told me once. "Just like he does everyone. We don't need all this. Henry, I'm happier when we are on our own." I should have listened to her.

'About a week after we arrived, strange things started to happen. At first I thought it was all in my imagination. But sometimes I would see Maggie talking to someone. A man. Oh she would deny it. Saying I was seeing things. There were no strange men on Pollitt land that weren't family. One night I saw her though. Out on the lawn, close to the pond. And the man put his arms around her and kissed her. Just like she was his wife and not mine!

'Of course I flew into a rage again. I wanted to kill him. But when I ran outside she was alone. After that I knew there was someone else in her life. She continues to deny it. But I saw it with my own eyes.'

'But you haven't found out who?' I said.

Henry shook his head, 'No. And no one else will talk. Not even Orlando. All he says is, "I told you not to bring her back here". I'm at my wit's end Kat. I don't know what to do. Every night Maggie is in my room, in my bed. But I can't think beyond the knowledge that she has a lover. I can't touch her no more. It makes me heart sick.'

'Henry,' I said. 'You've been a total idiot. Maggie isn't having an affair. She clearly loves you.'

'I know what I saw Kat. How do you explain her being in the arms of another man? Even if the cowardly-dog keeps hiding himself from me and the world.'

'I can't explain it. Yet. But I will. And I also know who might be able to explain some of what's happening here. Can you take me into town? I need to send a telegram. I think Pepper and I are going to need some help and advice from a well-read friend of ours.'

11

It was early evening on the fifth day of our visit. I was standing on the balcony when I saw a large balloon, made out of thick coarse canvas, silhouetted against the sunset. I hurried to Pepper's door and knocked on. It took him a moment to answer but as he opened the door he looked beyond me noticing immediately what I had come to tell him.

'Martin's here,' he said. 'I hope your new in-laws aren't too unhappy about having another visitor sprung upon them.'

'They will be too polite to complain,' I said. 'Mother might not like it though …'

We had spent the day examining the layout of the house. The room that I thought I'd seen the day before didn't exist. Or appeared not to. But I was certain of what I had seen and so Pepper and I began to ask questions. Was there a room ever there? Who might have occupied it? Why would it be sealed up and hidden?

106

Of course we didn't ask these questions of the family or the servants. Just discussed the possibilities together, wondering what we could do and who to approach without making our curiosity too obvious.

'Kat?' Mother called.

She too had come out onto the balcony. Maybe she had heard me knock on Pepper's door and was wondering why I would go to his room like that. Her constant chaperoning lately was beginning to irritate me. Pepper and I had been finding it extremely difficult to be alone and to talk lately. If Mother wasn't there, then Sally was, and when both of them were absent I was still being courted by Orlando.

That evening we were all dressed for the evening party. This was the formal wedding evening for Maggie and Henry and many of the local landowners and gentry had been invited, as well as some distant relations of the Pollitts, to help them celebrate the marriage, even if it was somewhat belated.

'I'm here,' I said.

Mother joined Pepper and I on the balcony and turned her head to see what we were looking at.

'Oh no!' she said. 'You didn't!'

'Didn't what, Mother?' I said.

'You didn't ask that gunslinger to come …'

'Martin is not a gunslinger, Mother … He's an inventor.'

Even so I smiled. I had an image of Martin weighed down with his steam-powered, clockwork and SunPan energy weapons in some backwater town, dark hair falling into his eyes as he squinted up towards the midday sun. Most women would see him as a romantic figure I suppose. I could also see why Mother worried about my relationship with him, as well as with Pepper. But, like Pepper, I knew Martin too well to become romantically involved with him. And … both of them knew me too. Despite her concerns we were not some obscene *ménage à trois*.

'You invited him,' Mother said again.

'We need his help,' I said.

'Whatever for?'

'I can't say at the moment. Best you don't know …'

Mother sighed and was just about to argue when Pepper chipped in. 'Mrs Lightfoot, would you like me to escort you and Sally down to the drawing room. A nice long drink of something cold and refreshing is just what we all need right now.

Mother was, as always, too well-mannered to argue with Pepper and so she let him take her arm, and he led her back to her room to fetch Sally. As they reached the door to her room, she turned and glowered at me. Mother's anger was something I could handle though. For now it was important to learn what kind of entity we were dealing with at Pollitt Plantation, and how to rid them of it as soon as possible. It was obvious to me, if not to anyone else, that somehow this thing was responsible for the rift between Maggie and Henry, and was indeed affecting our behaviour too.

By the time Pepper returned from escorting Mother and Sally downstairs, Martin's airship was hovering above the lawn.

It was an imposing thing. The basket had been replaced with what could only be described as a small galleon-like ship.

The canvas balloon above, which was double the width of the ship it carried, made the whole thing stand as tall as the house. As we walked across the lawn to greet Martin as he landed I looked back at the building and noticed that the airship – and truly it was more deserving of that name now than it had ever been – actually threw a shadow over the house.

This close I could see that the 'ship' was covered by a thin layer of highly polished metal over what had first appeared to be wooden planks. Instead of the usual invisible nails, the metal planks were secured by large rivets. On deck, I noticed that the control box, which was housed below the balloon and contained the various dials and levers which Martin used to control his flight, was much larger than its predecessor and had some additional switches and buttons too. Either side of the balloon were two large engines that were probably activated by the controls when the steam engine producing the hot air that pumped into the balloon wasn't enough. Martin stood at the helm, turning the wheel just as he might have had he been on the high seas. There was even a kind of rudder that moved in the air with each small turn.

Of course the machine was noisy. And steam poured out from a long, thick pipe that was attached to the side of the ship. It produced almost as much engine noise and pollution as the steam train that we had travelled across the country on. But as Martin dropped those final few feet to the ground, the engine silenced and the steam came out of the pipe in one final hiss.

'You've made some changes,' I called up as Martin

leaned over the starboard bow and saluted.

'I did make a few tweaks,' said Martin.

'What on Earth is going on?' said Big Momma as she came out from the drawing room onto the lawn. I saw that Mother was looking out from the room. She was flushed red as though she were embarrassed by the whole situation – which I suppose she was. I knew then that another long and stern conversation was coming my way soon.

I smiled at Big Momma though, determined to make light of Martin's appearance. She was wearing a bright red gown that had the widest skirt I had ever seen – and the lowest neckline. She looked very pretty to be honest and it was difficult not to note the contrast between her and Mother once more. I wondered if it was just a personality thing. Big Momma was very vivacious, whereas Mother tended to be very reserved all the time and rarely let herself relax and enjoy anything.

'Big Momma,' I said. 'This is a friend of ours, Martin Crewe. I hope you don't mind. He's practically family and I invited him over.'

Martin lowered a rope ladder over the side and climbed down with practiced agility. He hammered some mooring ropes into the ground – although the ship appeared to be heavy enough to keep itself on the floor – and then he came over to allow me to properly introduce him. Fortunately he wasn't wearing *all* of his weapons. This might at least appease Mother in some small way. But he did have an ordinary looking holster belt and gun slung over his slim hips. I suspected that the weapon inside the holster was anything but ordinary though.

'I do hope you don't mind my parking the Airship here,' Martin said to Big Momma as he bowed over her hand.

Big Momma was completely charmed by his dark good looks, just as she had been by Pepper's blond handsomeness, and so I knew immediately that all would be well. In fact she was rather pleased by Martin's impromptu appearance as she flirted with him outrageously.

'Why this is so exciting! Two handsome young men to make the evening fun. And this thing ... this ... *Airship*? I have never seen a ship on dry land like this before. It's fascinating. Why I think all of the guests may find it quite a talking point. My goodness it actually flies too doesn't it? Do come in Mr Crewe, I will tell Isaac to set another place at the table. The ball guests will be arriving soon and we have a wedding to celebrate.'

'If I may?' said Martin. 'I did bring something more appropriate to wear for the evening.' (Another point in Martin's favour that really couldn't hurt where Mother's approval was concerned. At least he would be dressed appropriately for the evening and she couldn't justify her continued disapproving frown.)

'You can use my room to change,' Pepper said.

It was all so formal, polite and yes ... that awful thing ... *proper*, that it irritated me somewhat. Part of me had wanted something different to happen. It amazed me how society people, when they were faced with something extreme and out of the ordinary, always reacted as though it was the most normal thing in the world. As if to say 'No. I'm not accepting this' was too awful to conceive.

I followed Pepper and Martin back up the external steps and onto the balcony.

'So, Martin. What is that metal around the hull?' I asked.

'It's tin. A little armour plating if you will ...'

'Tin?' said Pepper. 'Canned-food-tin?'

'Well not quite, but sort of. This has been treated in such a way that it's far stronger than the cans of course. You wouldn't be able to put a knife through this and open it! But it is still as light. A very resourceful material when weight is an issue. Plus it also helps collect energy to send into the sun panels. It's not quite strong enough to run the ship yet – I'm still working on that – but it does run the lighting and heating system on board.'

'I want to know what the new dials do ...' I said linking his arm. Strangely being this friendly with Martin always felt a little more natural than touching Pepper did. I wasn't sure why, but I was aware of it as we walked back to our rooms. Martin felt more like ... a brother to me than Pepper for some reason. Even though I could trust Pepper just the same.

I loved Martin's inventions. I always liked to know exactly how they worked. Though sometimes he kept some of his secrets to himself.

'The new dials on the control box are a surprise. But I promise to show you when we need them. Now, tell me about your problem here ...'

I was about to start explaining everything about the ghost and the vanishing bedroom when Mother came up onto the balcony.

'Kat. I think it will be far more appropriate if you came downstairs now and joined the family to greet the arriving guests. I'm sure Mr Pepper will be able to help Mr Crewe change for dinner.'

'Yes Mother,' I sighed.

Sometimes it was just no fun being female.

12

'This is where the room was?' asked Martin.

It was very late when I met Pepper and Martin at the end of the landing, in the very spot where I had seen the door and the mysterious nephilim child. The party had gone well, the guests had long since left and the Pollitt family and servants had all retired.

'After that, the phantom tried to suffocate Kat,' Pepper explained.

'It's dangerous then,' Martin said.

I explained its lack of matter, but how I had still felt 'something' as I fought it.

'Ectoplasm,' Martin said and then, when Pepper and I looked bemused, he went on to explain all that he knew. 'It's a kind of substance that is generated by spirits when they try to communicate with the living. I did a study on it last year. Went to many a séance. Most were frauds to be honest though

114

... then there was this one spirit that came through. I won't bore you with the details but it left behind a mass of this stuff all over the medium that channelled it. Like a clear, sticky gel.'

'It felt like that,' I said. 'But the next day there was nothing on my hands.'

'It dissipates after a few hours,' Martin said. 'Which is why I couldn't use it as I had wanted to.'

'What could you use it for?' I asked.

'Ectoplasm is pure energy, Kat. It's the fuel the spirits use to cross the dimension between life and death. Can you imagine being able to harness that power?'

'You've lost us both on that one,' Pepper said. 'Dimension?'

'Think of it as another world ... that runs and lives parallel to ours.'

'How do you know all this?' I asked.

'It's a theory I have really. About life and death that may explain our relationship with religion. Death is merely just another place. It is ethereal and we are corporeal. But once our physical body has worn out we join that realm and as we move onto the other dimension this one becomes closed to us.'

'But then how does that truly explain spirits and phantom, ghosts if you like?' I asked.

Martin explained his thoughts as simply as he could. He believed that sometimes the dimensions became thin and sometimes we could see the other one, or at least some people could. I didn't fully understand his theory, but it gave me food for thought. What I did understand was that sometimes these ghosts or spirits didn't want to cross over into the other realm and clung onto this one, even though they couldn't really live in it anymore.

Martin studied the wall once more. 'There is no sign at all of a door. But that doesn't mean there isn't one. Sometimes our eyes refuse to see what our hearts know is real.'

'I did *see* it though,' I whispered.

'I think this child is probably a ghost. The fact that you heard its tears may mean you are gifted in mediumship, Kat. You're one of the few genuine people who can see into that other dimension.'

'The child is *dead* then?' I said.

It was horrible to imagine even for a moment that the child I had spoken to wasn't alive. He had seemed so ... vital. Even though he was a nephilim and had boasted of trying to drown his own sister, I felt that the boy had been truly unhappy. I'd been drawn to help him, but something had tried to stop me, which made me wonder if something else was holding the child captive for its own designs. Perhaps the boy wasn't evil at all. The jury was still out on that one though. And it wasn't like me to feel any sympathy for anything that was associated with a demon or the Darkness.

'I think perhaps what I'm saying,' Martin continued. 'Is that you could probably bring this door forth anytime you wanted. It might not exist in the real world. But it does in the ethereal one.'

'Do you think that I might have crossed into this world when I walked over the threshold?' I asked, feeling decidedly uneasy as I recalled the lack of external normal sounds when I was in the room.

'I think that you crossed over, but maybe not physically. I really can't be sure though.'

'It felt real …' I said.

I had seen many things over the past few years but I was struggling to come to terms with Martin's theories. Although I was willing to experiment with idea that I could possibly control this newfound skill and open the door again, I wasn't really sure it was possible. It still felt as though some other force had made it happen, and I was merely the person that was chosen for the revelation.

I looked at the wall long and hard. Then ran my fingers over where I thought the door had been. I tried to concentrate, I really did. But I felt nothing which only confirmed to me that I didn't possess any particular power to see through our world into another.

'It's useless,' I said after a while. 'All I see is the wall.'

'Maybe we need to recreate the events of the evening,' Pepper suggested.

'How are we going to do that?' I asked.

'You were relaxed and sleepy,' Martin prompted.

I shook my head. 'No. I was jerked awake by a scream. I was in full battle mode. Gun in hand. I wasn't sleepy or even groggy.'

We all fell silent and contemplated the dilemma. There was no way we could possibly recreate the scenario. Especially if it had not occurred by accident, or a series of events, but was by the design of something we did not understand.

'I'll have another look in the daylight,' Martin suggested.

I left Martin and Pepper at the door to Pepper's room and walked silently down the corridor but as I reached my door I heard the muffled sobs once more.

The servants had made up a bed for Martin in Pepper's room and so I hurried back and knocked on their door as quietly as I could. There was no answer, but the sobs were louder now and so I gave up and hurried back towards the corridor's end.

I stared at the wall. It was *just* a wall, but as I pressed my ear against it I could hear muted tears. I felt impotent and frustrated again. The child was locked in there. Had he really tried to murder his sister as he said? Or was that some form of bravado? Suddenly I began to believe that it was. I recalled again the smiling face, it had been a contrived expression. He had been trying to make himself appear frightening. Or maybe I just wanted to believe that he wasn't a monster.

I glanced back towards Pepper's room. Neither of the men had emerged, which was strange because there hadn't been enough time for them to fall asleep. I went back. Knocked louder. There was still no answer and so I decided to try the door instead. The handle turned in my fingers, but as the door opened I realised that this wasn't Pepper's room at all.

I found myself face to face once more with the nephilim child, sitting in the large bed, tears in his eyes.

'Oh it's you!' he said.

'Are you all right?' I asked. I stood awkwardly in the

corridor looking inwards.

'I never expected to see you again,' said the boy.

'I've been trying to get back in.'

'I'm sorry if my eyes scared you.'

He was different this time somehow. The child felt relieved that I was there it seemed.

'It's not your fault,' I said. I felt an intense wave of compassion. He looked so lost. So forlorn. Why hadn't I realised that last time?

I stood on the threshold, warily considering whether to cross again. Outside of the room I could hear the sounds of the sleeping occupants of the house. The steady creak of the timbers cooling in the night air.

I closed my eyes for a moment and took a deep breath. I wasn't armed. I had no way at all of defending myself if something went wrong. But as I looked over the threshold I met the boy's eyes. The tears were drying on his cheeks.

'You didn't really try to drown your sister did you?' I asked.

The boy looked down at his hands, then shook his head. 'Of course not. I would never do that. I love her.'

I made the decision and crossed the threshold. Sound disappeared again but my senses were far more acute this time, and I was determined to take any clues I could back to Pepper and Martin. This room had a hollow feel to it. Like the open eves of a church, or the echo found in old ruins. The emptiness was palpable, and impossible. The room was full of furniture. There was a soft carpet beneath my feet.

Thick curtains covered the windows. This vacant atmosphere couldn't be real. Or could it?

I blinked.

The oil lamp suddenly extinguished and darkness filled the room. I stopped walking.

I blinked again. The light returned and the boy was staring at me, wide-eyed and curious again, as though he were seeing me for the first time.

I blinked once more. The room now looked like a bare attic space. The bed was still there, but empty and the sheets were rotten, and moth-eaten. The boy was gone.

I opened and closed my eyes and once more the child and room reappeared.

'What's happening?' I said.

'You see me don't you?' The boy pleaded.

'Yes. Of course.'

I walked over to the bed and sat down on the edge to wedge myself in *this* present. 'How long have you been here?'

The boy looked up with his strange amber eyes and smiled at me. 'You're nice. You aren't at all like he said you would be …'

'Who said?'

'Callon. He is angry with me.'

'Callon?'

'He's my father,' said the boy.

'Oh? I thought your father was Michel …' I said because part of me still wanted to believe that this child was one of Amelia and Michel Beaugard's. But of course he wasn't. It had been a ridiculous notion.

The door behind me remained open and I wasn't afraid of the child at all. I felt strangely safe, unlike two nights ago when my strength evaporated in this very room. But things had changed. The boy had changed somehow as though the thing that had tainted him was gone. Had been taken away. But that thought was too peculiar, and impossible to consider. Other than his eyes he seemed perfectly normal.

'What are you?' I asked suddenly. 'Spirit? Demon?'

The boy frowned. 'I'm Dando.'

The thought occurred to me that the room and the light were all echoes that were somehow reaching out to me. I was seeing something that no longer existed in my world. And it scared me more than the demon that had tried to suffocate the life out of me because it meant that what Martin had said about dimensions, may actually be true. And if we could see into that other world, then surely they could see us. Who knew what a malignant phantom was capable of if it found a way into our world.

I felt cold suddenly. A dark shadow fell across the bed and Dando yelped.

'You'd better leave!' he hissed. But I knew already it was too late.

I turned around to face the demon that had been haunting Pollitt Plantation.

A thick miasma shifted and turned as the creature began to take shape. On impulse I reached out and grabbed Dando's hand. I was afraid for him and, even though my rational mind said it was impossible, I would try to take him from this awful hell-hole back into the real world.

Dando's small fingers trembled in my hand, but they felt warm and I was reassured that he wasn't the same as this monster.

'Father ...' the boy gasped.

So this was Callon. A demon from some terrible realm. How had he found his way here? How had he managed to couple with a human female in order to make this poor confused boy?

Dando slid from the covers and cowered against me. His body burned like a small furnace, pushing away the awful, icy cold that Callon's shadow induced.

'What do you want with this child?' I said, hoping that perhaps there was a chance to reason with it. 'Why are you keeping him here?'

'Get out!' roared Callon, his voice like thunder.

'Not without him ...' I said.

'I can't leave,' the boy whispered. 'It's not possible.'

Callon's features were slowly taking shape. His face was a charred and blackened skull. Empty eye sockets lit by a yellow, burning light of pure evil. His form took on a more solid substance. Shaped in the height and form of a man, with two arms, two legs, I could see how at a distance he could be mistaken for one. But the smell that came from him – like pig skin which had been roasted on a spit for far too long – caught under my nostrils and made me gag. He smelt and looked burnt, but a cold aura rolled from him like a frozen mist.

I shrank back with the boy. I had seen some demon forms, but none were quite like this. How could this thing possibly inhabit our world? How could it ever be able to convince any woman to see it as a potential lover?

I glanced back at Dando. He was frowning but no longer seemed afraid of the figure. When my eyes returned to Callon, I saw a man before me. A beautiful man that reminded me so much of Orlando Pollitt that I was stunned. This was how he seduced. He could change his image like any other demon. But I knew from experience that it took energy for them to sustain a human form, or a glamour. What did this monster feed on in order to be able to look like this?

I slid forward on the bed, pulling the child with me.

Yes, children and babies were slowly becoming my weakness when faced with demons it seemed. I weighed up my options for a moment. The door to the landing was still open. I could grab Dando and run for it. It was likely that Callon would try to stop us however.

I recalled the heavy pressure, the suffocating feeling that this monster had forced on me just two nights ago. I hadn't been able to fight him. I didn't think I could now and so my options for surviving this encounter were rapidly diminishing.

'You need to leave,' the boy whispered in my ear. 'You can't take me. *They* trapped me here. I can't ever go back.'

I pulled him onto my knee. He was so small and frail and I hugged him as though I were his mother. The urge to protect him was so strong that my other instincts were at odds with it.

'I'm not leaving you here,' I said.

Callon laughed. 'That was what his mother said too. But she had to settle with what was left after the ritual.'

'Ritual? What ritual? Did someone sacrifice this boy to you?'

Callon's handsome face crumpled. He was clearly finding the glamour difficult to sustain, or maybe I could see through it as much in this place as I could in my own world. His hideous visage, accompanied by the charred odour, fell back over his form like a black curtain dropping over a stage. The stretched skin was slick, as though smeared with burned goose fat, and it dripped from him with a steady thud, like a tap that hadn't been turned off properly.

I stood up with the boy clasped in my arms and moved towards the door. Callon blocked me.

'He *can't* leave here …' he said.

'Do you want him to suffer like this?' I asked. 'Surely if he's your son …'

Callon's form deteriorated further. This time back into thick black smoke. It billowed in impotent fury and beat against me with failing strength. The pressure I'd felt before wasn't there. It was as though his energy and resources were depleted.

My resolve to remove Dando from this otherworldly room strengthened. I felt no fear of this thing now, and the shadow of darkness, as well as the cold emanating from the demon, fell away as I progressed to the door. But as I reached the threshold, the boy was pulled from my grasp by some invisible force. His small body was thrown back onto the bed, like a small doll, discarded by a spoilt child.

Dando cried out in fear, but as I tried to run back to him once more, I found myself propelled outside and I fell into the corridor.

The door closed and faded from sight as though it had never existed. I remained on my hands and knees staring at the wall and realising I was indeed back at the end of the corridor and nowhere near Pepper's room.

'What the devil is going on?' I said struggling to my feet.

I stared at the perfect wall, pressed my ear back where I had found the doorway, but this time no sound issued from inside. Dando was beyond my reach, and the realm he inhabited had expelled me like a drunk being thrown from a brothel.

I accepted the flask of brandy and sipped cautiously, letting the warming fluid course down my throat.

'This will steady your nerves,' Pepper insisted.

'My nerves are fine. Honestly.'

I was sat on a chair in Pepper's room. It was still full night and Pepper and Martin had heard me crash back into the corridor. They had opened Pepper's door to find me lying stunned at the end of the corridor. I also discovered that to them it had been only moments since we had all parted.

'I can't believe we didn't hear you knock,' said Martin. 'We had only just closed the door when we heard you.'

Of course to me a good half an hour had passed. Maybe

longer. I just wasn't sure, but I knew it wasn't just seconds.

'It's obvious that the forces at work here didn't want our interference. Kat must have crossed the portal to this new dimension as she left us. She was probably never actually knocking at our door at all …' Martin continued.

'My head is reeling with all this. I had the boy, Dando, in my hands, Callon couldn't stop me, but something else did.'

'He did tell you he *couldn't* leave …' Pepper said but I didn't need the reminder.

'I'm intrigued about this ritual …' Martin said. 'Religion fascinates me by its accidental accuracy.'

'What do you mean?' I asked.

'Well most of the ceremonies that take place in a church, for example, come directly from our ancestors who didn't believe in the God we worship now. Their beliefs surrounded nature. The early druids performed sacraments that were about worshipping forces we no longer understand, but they did.'

'Isn't that linked to Witchcraft?' Pepper said.

Martin laughed. 'Not the way you mean, no. But some magic was employed, yes. But the rituals were carried down, though changed somewhat. These ceremonies are now often performed without the slightest understanding of their true significance. Or their power …'

I placed the flask back into Pepper's hands.

'I need to sleep. This has all been too much for me.'

'Perhaps you would be safer here,' Pepper said. 'Last time that monster – Callon was he called? – tried to suffocate you.'

'I know. But he has no strength to do it right now. Even

if he wanted to. I doubt that in his current state he can even cross over into our realm.'

Martin and Pepper exchanged a look that showed their mutual concern.

'We have to find out where it draws its energy from and make sure it doesn't return to full strength then,' Pepper said.

'Let me know when you figure that one out. It is the one thing that keeps running through my brain that I can't make any sense of,' I said. 'Goodnight.'

I stood and walked, weary, battered and bruised back to the door.

13

I woke to another bright and beautiful day. I had slept solidly and my pocket watch told me that it was well into the morning.

The wedding feasting was over. The family would be expecting Mother, Sally and I to depart soon, but I knew that I couldn't leave until I had solved the mystery of the demon at Pollitt Plantation. Callon was dangerous, but there was clearly something else here too.

I hurriedly dressed and made my way downstairs and to the orangery, where I found Big Momma sipping China tea from porcelain teacups. She was alone.

'Good morning Kat,' she said cheerfully.

She looked tired though, and unusually worn as though the week of festivities had finally taken their toll.

'Good morning,' I said. 'How are you this fine day?'

'Well to tell you the truth, I didn't sleep too well. I guess it was all the excitement over the wedding party. It was quite a strain. I wanted everything to be so perfect for Maggie and Henry.'

'It was perfect,' I said, remembering the magnificent food, the flowing wine and the happy crowd of neighbours, family and friends who had attended.

Even Maggie and Henry had appeared to enjoy themselves. Although I knew they were both excellent at hiding how they really felt around Big Momma and Big Daddy. I had danced with Orlando too, but I barely remembered the conversation we'd had because for me the evening had been tense, one of waiting until Martin, Pepper and I could finally do our secret research.

'I had strange dreams also …' Big Momma continued. 'Like something was choking me.' She shuddered. 'Awful.'

'That is awful,' I said, suddenly alert. 'Have you … had that dream before?'

'Oh it's silly. I'm just getting caught up on the superstition of … the blacks. They believe in all that stuff you know. Evil spirits. This thing called voodoo or something …'

I studied her carefully, feeling for the first time that I was actually seeing her. That she was opening up to tell me something that would help us figure out what was happening.

'It doesn't sound silly … I have heard of some bizarre religions … but the dream … it's happened before?'

Big Momma raised her cup to her lips and sipped the tea. 'Well … not to me. But Maggie was always talking about a dream like that when she was young. And some of the servants have been known to have disturbed nights that they believed was real. But you know how they are …'

I didn't know. Not at all. But I felt I was on the cusp of learning something vital. And though she delivered this information in a casual way, Big Momma was deliberately trying to tell me something.

'Now you feel weak? Tired? A little drained?' I queried.

Big Momma nodded. 'I just need better rest.'

It occurred to me that maybe this Callon-thing drained energy from people like an incubus might. I wanted to ask her more but as the servants came in with the freshly cooked breakfast, Big Momma changed the subject. I didn't get another opportunity to question her after that because Amelia appeared with her three obnoxious boys in tow.

After breakfast I left Big Momma to go in search of my companions. Mother and Sally had taken to going for walks in the morning, always returning for lunch with the family, and so I wasn't overly worried about them at the time.

Outside the airship remained in situ, dwarfing the house, glowing in the sunshine. I touched the metal on the side of the hull and discovered it was warm, but not hot. Then, I slipped off my day skirt, revealing my tight breeches beneath, and climbed up onto the deck via the rope ladder that still hung over the side. I was sure Martin would be here, but also I was curious to see the new ship and the dials that he had been so secretive about.

As I jumped down onto the deck I looked over the horizon and saw the sun drifting beneath a thick black cloud. Out to sea the daylight was plummeting as storm clouds gathered. So far we'd had nothing but beautiful weather since we arrived, but now a storm was brewing. Although it looked as though it would be many hours before it reached us.

I shrugged, then looked around the deck, wondering where to explore first. I felt that familiar wave of excitement as I knew I was on the cusp of learning more about Martin's wonderful invention.

'Miss Kat? Are you up on that thing?'

I hurried along the deck and looked over the side to see Orlando standing below.

'Hello,' I said.

'Can I come up?'

'No. I'll come down to you. I was looking for Martin. I don't suppose you have seen him and Pepper have you?'

I didn't think that Martin would like having Orlando on board his ship and so I climbed back over the rail and onto the rope ladder. When I reached the bottom I realised that Orlando was a little bit confused by my lack of dress. And somewhat embarrassed because he could now see the shape of my legs and hips in the tight breeches.

I picked up my skirt from the grass where I had left it.

'No. I'm afraid I haven't seen them,' Orlando said, trying to hide his confusion. 'But the horses are ready.'

'Horses?'

'Yes. Last night, when we were talking, you said you'd like to take a ride around the plantation ... but if you've changed your mind ...'

With all of the excitement from the night before I had

completely forgotten the conversation I'd had with Orlando.

'Oh no! That's fine. In fact that is a really good idea.'

'Perhaps you would …' he said.

'No, this is perfect for riding in,' I said. But I knew that Mother might not be too impressed if she saw me like this here. She had, in fact, ordered me to leave the breeches behind. But I had put them inside my carpet bag, just in case.

'I'll be right back,' I said to Orlando.

I hurried up the external stairs, onto the balcony and into my room where I deposited my skirt on top of the bed.

By the time I reached the stables, Orlando was waiting. He was petting a horse that had black and white patches on it. I had never seen one like this before. I was used to the full colour Bays, or Chestnuts, that were preferred by the Hansom cab drivers in New York. This was a beautiful animal though. It appeared to be sturdier than the horses I had ridden in Central Park.

'These were favoured by the Apache Indians,' Orlando explained. 'Since you were dressed differently I took the liberty of having the saddle changed from side to normal.'

'Thank you.'

'She's called Felina. And she's got a real sweet temperament,' Orlando explained.

Orlando helped me up into the saddle and I petted Felina's neck as I talked to her. Then, once he was up on his own mount – a slightly bigger brown and white patched stallion called Aron – Orlando turned the reins and led us away from the paddock.

132

As we rode away from the house it crossed my mind to be concerned that I hadn't seen Pepper or Martin at all yet, but of course my friends were more than likely trying to find out all they could about the Plantation and the family history.

Orlando took off across the flat landscape and Aron's long legs galloped away. Immediately Felina, as though she had been trained to follow Aron, picked up her pace and I found myself galloping after him. The wind ripped through the lose bun I had carelessly twisted my hair into earlier, and I felt the pins coming lose. My hair fell down in waves over my shoulders, but I really didn't mind. The air felt wonderful. I had almost forgotten how good it was to ride on open land.

Orlando slowed as we reached the edge of the cotton plants. A crew of workers were picking the cotton as we trotted by. I was surprised to see white men and women among them, working side by side with the black workers.

'Every harvest we need a little more help, so we draft in anyone willing to put in a hard day's work,' Orlando explained as though he could read my thoughts.

'That's very progressive of you,' I said.

We passed on, out towards the worker's village, skirting around the edge, but not passing the small huts this time as we reached the side of a dense patch of forest.

'I want to show you something,' Orlando said. He nudged Aron forward and into the trees.

The vegetation thickened as we weaved slowly through it. Felina traversed the terrain, stepping over large, over-grown roots and fallen branches with sure-footed confidence. It was as though she often came here and knew the way without thinking. And yet there was no natural, worn path, and the way appeared to be for the most part untraveled.

'Where are we going?' I asked.

Orlando smiled over his shoulder. 'You'll like this … I promise.'

We rode on a while longer, and I began to feel some concern about finding my way back if I were to have the misfortune to lose Orlando. Up ahead I saw a slice of sun cutting through the trees, which indicated that they were finally thinning.

We came into a clearing and there, much to my surprise, was a table set with food and Isaac standing by to wait on us.

'I thought we might have a nice lunch together,' Orlando said. He brought Aron to a stop, jumped down, tied his reins to one of the trees and turned to help me. I jumped down myself and once again I saw that slight flush of embarrassment cross Orlando's features. It amazed me that he was so shy.

'This is nice,' I said, but I felt slightly nervy. Once more my comfort zone had been breached, and I felt my senses being bombarded by this overly attractive, sensitive and charismatic man. The most confusing thing for me was that I had to keep reminding myself that Orlando was half-demon. He couldn't be liked. He couldn't be trusted. But still, despite myself, I did like him. It wasn't like me at all. Yet when I was around him I felt safe. It was peculiar. And unnatural to me. Especially when I knew there was something so completely wrong with this place.

It began to worry me that other than the small silver

dagger in my boot, I was completely unarmed. Even so I hid my feelings as I took a seat at the small table and let Isaac fill my plate with a selection of fresh cheeses and some fruit. On the table was a carafe of wine, two glasses, and a bowl containing cut up pieces of bread.

I ate slowly because it wasn't that long since we had eaten breakfast and by the time we finished, and had sipped a glass of crisp white wine, the sky above us was darkening.

I had of course forgotten completely that there was a storm on its way, and it arrived far quicker than I had anticipated it would.

Drops of rain splattered the table.

'Oh my!' said Orlando. 'I had better get you under cover, Miss Kat. I'm so sorry!'

I laughed. 'You have nothing to be sorry about, you didn't make this storm happen.'

We climbed back on our horses.

'What about Isaac?' I said as I saw him clearing away the plates and glasses into a small barrow.

'Don't worry, this isn't that far from the house. I just took you the long way around so that we would benefit more from the ride.'

I nodded and urged Felina back through the trees, following Orlando as he pointed Aron in what I hoped was the right direction for the house.

A roll of thunder echoed above us as the forest thickened again. The brief glimpse I had of the sky showed a thick black cloud drifting over us, just before the forest became as dark as night.

Felina stumbled a little, her feet now unsure, and her calm temperament became jittery.

'Perhaps we should walk the horse through?' I called to Orlando but he didn't hear me as the rain started to beat down in earnest.

Within seconds, and despite the cover of the trees, I was drenched and I felt the ground beneath Felina's feet become slippery and dangerous.

'Orlando!' I called out.

He was much farther ahead of me now and didn't look back when I called. I began to wonder if we were going to make it back to the house at all.

The rain beat down into my eyes and it was difficult to see. Felina slipped again, and I made a decision to rein her in and climb down. I pushed the rain from my face, forced my long wet hair out of my eyes and began to lead Felina through the mud and thick roots, towards the set of trees that I had last seen Orlando pass. I couldn't see his figure at all now but I wondered if he could still see me if he glanced back, and if he had noticed I had dismounted.

Felina tugged at the reins as another clap of thunder, closer this time, frightened her. I coaxed her forward, weaving the leather around my hand to prevent the reins from slipping from my wet fingers. As we reached the next tree, I pulled her close underneath its wide branches and once again wiped the rain away from my face. I petted her as I looked around trying to get my bearings. The forest was still too dense to see beyond it, and I couldn't see Orlando anywhere.

A flash of lightning lit up the trees. Felina mewed and twisted, but I yanked back on the bit, bringing her under control before she became too agitated. She didn't pull back, but didn't fully settle either. I was surprised that a storm could affect her so much, but there was something unusual about this one. It was so dark it was almost night. Hard to imagine we could go from such fine weather to this in such a short space of time.

I debated, waiting to see if Orlando realised that he had lost me, but then with Felina's increasing irritation, I decided it might be best to keep moving.

Another flash of lightning lit the sky through the branches overhead, and I thought I saw movement in the trees to my left. Surely Orlando had gone that way. I pulled Felina onwards. I could see horse tracks in the mud now and so followed. The forest began to thin, and with relief I approached another clearing.

14

I slowed as I grew closer.

The clearing was full of people. Mostly the black servants, but I saw an occasional white face among them. Big Daddy was there, holding centre stage as he sat on a huge, roughly carved wooden throne, like a King overlooking his courtiers.

The head house servant, Isaac, was wearing a long white robe and was carrying a staff that was almost as tall as he was. The staff had bones tied to and hanging from it and they clattered together as Isaac shook his wrist. The congregation, for now I realised that was what they were, grew quiet.

In the distance I could hear the beating of a drum. The same beat and sound I had heard almost every night since we arrived. I'd heard of these practices among the blacks, of the rituals they brought with them, how they honoured barbaric, ancient gods that demanded sacrifices. What was it Big Momma had called it? *Voodoo*. That was right. This was something to do with their superstitions.

Felina nudged me from behind, but I stayed where we were under cover of the trees and tied her up under the best shelter I could find. Some instinct made me realise that it would be unwise to reveal my presence. Unobserved, I crept back to the clearing, crouched down in the long grass and watched the proceedings.

It struck me that there was no rain in the clearing, yet it continued to come down on me where I hid in the forest. In fact the grass and trees and people in this area were all dry, even though thick cloud still loomed above.

The drum began to beat faster and louder, and the people, including Big Daddy, took up a chant that was incomprehensible to me. One of the servant girls I had seen previously began to dance before Isaac, she was no longer wearing her uniform, but wore instead some kind of loin cloth, her naked breasts were barely covered by a crude necklace that appeared to be made of small bones that looked as sharp as the teeth of a shark. Isaac shook the staff over her as though he were giving some form of blessing, and she danced away to the rhythmic beat of the drum. Soon more of the girls came, one after another, all semi-naked as they danced, twisting and turning beneath the rattling bones of Isaac's staff.

When this part of their strange communion was done, the men came, one after another and finally Isaac went up to Big Daddy and shook the bones over him.

It was then that I noticed that Big Daddy was not quite himself. He didn't respond to the ritual as the others did, he merely stared ahead, as though he was sleeping with his eyes open.

Isaac spoke but the language he used was not something I recognised. It was something primal, guttural at times, high-pitched at others. More a collection of sounds that made no sense at all than a language. The servants seemed to understand him though, or at least they responded in a way that indicated some level of comprehension for the ritual.

My maid servant, Milly, stepped forward. She was carrying a chicken, and it clucked and twisted, unusable wings flapping as though it knew what fate was facing it. She followed Isaac as he led her in dance-like steps around the group. All the time the chicken tried to escape from her fingers, but she somehow managed to hold on.

As they once more reached the foot of Big Daddy's makeshift throne, one of the men danced forward with a large curved knife. With every step he swung the knife around his body with practised ease as he gyrated to the staccato drum rhythm until he reached the foot of the throne.

Another man stepped forward holding a small pedestal that supported a large bowl. Isaac caught the chicken by its feet, pulled it free of Milly's fingers and it fell, head pointing downwards, wings still flapping. He held the bird over the bowl with one hand. With the other he took the curved knife. Before I could react he severed the head from the bird and its decapitated body jerked and wriggled as though it were still alive. Blood splashed over Big Daddy who remained unmoved by the scene. Then Isaac gave the knife back to the young man who had brought it, and he now used his other hand to still the jerking of the dead bird while he captured the remains of the blood in the bowl.

The tempo of the drum picked up. An echo of sound shifted through the air and the clouds above began to clear. Slanted shafts of light cut through and illuminated the clearing. Then the congregation danced once more around the bowl as Isaac dipped his fingers in the blood and smeared the forehead of each of his disciples with the ichor.

I didn't know what to do at this point. The sacrifice of a bird was clearly to satisfy some strange belief and didn't horrify me. I could also sense no malice in the practice. There was a kind of beauty in the proceedings that led me to believe they weren't intending anything evil. The sunlight reassured me because the Darkness and its hordes always shunned light. The people here, however, seemed to embrace it as they danced around. But I didn't like the way Big Daddy appeared to be absent, even though he was physically present. He made no move at anytime, which indicated that perhaps a drug was being used on him, to make him compliant. Or that he was under some form of hypnosis.

I looked again around the group. I was sure that all of them were human, but I had only ever known supernaturals to be really capable of using mesmerism on their victims. It was not a skill that humans could employ to any particular effect, and certainly not as deeply as this was. Then another figure, a woman dressed in a robe, came from the other side of the clearing. I hadn't noticed her standing there because the robe was tones of green and browns and had somehow merged with the forest backdrop. She approached the pedestal and kneeled. Isaac dipped his fingers once more in the bowl and the woman threw back the hood of her robe.

It was Maggie.

I almost stood and revealed myself then, but I held back. This was a story that might play out to give me some information. Maggie was not hypnotised and in some trance-like state, she was fully alert and aware of what she was doing.

'Miss Maggie do you accept the help of the congregation to help protect your unborn child from the demon's spawn?' Isaac said, his voice reaching me clearly.

'Will it make it *leave*?' Maggie asked.

'We cannot make the demon leave, Miss Maggie. That is not a power in our hands. But we can protect you and your children.'

Maggie nodded as though resigned to some fate she had no control over.

'I accept your help,' she said.

Isaac took up the bone-laden staff once more and began to dance around Maggie. Her shoulders slumped and she dropped her head as though in prayer. Then Isaac's followers each took up the staff and imparted their strange blessing.

The rain in the forest stopped sometime during the ceremony. I waited for the proceedings to end and for Isaac and his people to leave. But I marked the way they went, particularly Maggie, who helped her dazed father from the throne as they headed back to what I hoped was in the direction of the main house.

I hurried back to Felina and began to walk her towards the clearing.

'Miss Kat!'

I turned and it was with some relief that I saw Orlando riding towards me.

'My goodness are you all right?' he asked. 'When I realised you were gone I circled back but couldn't find you.'

'I'm fine. I just took shelter from the rain,' I said, but I was confused and unnerved by what I had seen. The whole thing had raised more questions than it had answered.

'Come, the exit is this way,' said Orlando. He pointed in the opposite direction to the clearing.

'I thought I saw a way through this way,' I said, feeling unsure. Maybe he was deliberately trying to lose me in the forest.

Orlando's eyes showed a moment of fear as I pointed towards the clearing. 'Not that way. I can't go that way.'

I studied him for a moment, noting the genuine horror in his face. Maybe he knew of the rituals and was appalled by them. Perhaps the time had come for me to stop being discrete and start asking questions?

'Orlando I just went this way and I saw …'

Orlando backed away from me. 'It's this way …' he insisted. 'I promise not to lose you again.'

'Orlando …' I said but I knew that to question him was useless. He looked truly terrified. And so I did the only thing I could do, I climbed back onto Felina and followed him.

Just a few moments later we were out of the forest and back on a dirt track road. As soon as she could Felina took up a gallop back towards the house. It was almost as though she couldn't wait to be back in the safety of the stable.

15

I was determined to get some answers from Maggie about what was going on. Enough was enough. This had been the strangest morning I had ever had. After I had removed my soaking clothing, dried my hair and changed into a comfortable day-dress I went in search of her. My first port of call was her room. I had decided that I would bring this all out in the open even if Henry was there.

I rapped firmly on the door and within a few moments Maggie answered. She looked normal. Well as normal as someone who had been smeared in chicken's blood less than an hour earlier could look.

'Are you alone?' I asked.

'Hi Kat, what's wrong?' Henry said coming up behind Maggie.

'I need to talk to you both.'

Maggie stepped back and let me into the room.

'I know something is wrong between you two,' I said.

Maggie began to protest immediately, but Henry merely bowed his head. He slumped down onto the edge of the bed and put aside the crutch.

'How's your leg?' I said remembering my manners.

'A little better. But you came here to talk – so let's talk,' Henry said.

'Henry, no …' Maggie said quietly. 'Really Kat, there's nothing wrong. We're happy. We love each other.'

'There's no denying you love each other, Maggie,' I said. 'But the problems you have stem from something in this house and I want to know what it is.'

Maggie shook her head in denial.

'I saw you today. In the clearing.'

'Oh my lord!' Maggie put her hand to her mouth, then glanced at Henry. 'I was trying to save our marriage.'

'You want to save our marriage? Then you need to start telling me the truth. I can't stand this anymore. *Who* is he?'

'I never betrayed you …'

'I saw you …' Henry interrupted.

'Henry, I think Maggie is telling you the truth. Pieces of this puzzle have been pulling themselves together all week, but there is one major player in this that I don't understand. It's time you told us everything you know Maggie. I don't believe anyone can help you until they understand the whole story. You may not know this, but Pepper, Martin and I have seen some very strange things in this world. I have a better understanding than most about the supernatural. I also know that the ritual you took part in today won't do a thing to protect you.'

'Ritual?' Henry said.

'Big Momma swears by the blacks' rituals. She says they helped her, when I was a child, when Orlando …'

'What about Orlando? What part does he play?' I asked.

'Orlando? Nothing. He wouldn't hurt a fly …'

'Tell me more about Orlando. When was he born?

Maggie laughed 'About five minutes before I was.'

'Five minutes?' I asked.

'Didn't you realise? Orlando and I are twins.'

'That's not possible …' I said.

'Well we don't look much alike, true. But we both came from Big Momma on the same night …'

A moment of clarity. The puzzle pieces slid into place as though goose fat had been smeared on them. If Orlando was a nephilim, and he and Maggie were twins, it made Maggie a nephilim also. But Maggie's eyes were normal. She seemed completely human.

I had always assumed that Big Momma had been seduced by a demon. Through my contact with the boy I had learnt that the demon was called Callon. I was certain he was also the father of Orlando, which explained Big Daddy's obvious rejection of Orlando. But – then Callon had to be Maggie's father also, didn't he?

'Maggie you need to tell me everything,' I said again. 'This all has to stop if you and Henry are to be happy again.'

'I'm not having an affair Henry,' Maggie said. 'But there

is something living in our house. It's a ghost. I can't believe I'm telling you this … you'll probably think I'm insane … but I have been aware of it ever since I was a child.'

Henry said nothing.

'It's true,' I said. 'I've seen it too. It also scared Sally our first night here. It's a demon by the name of Callon and it tried to kill me a few nights ago.'

'Callon? So that is what he's called …' Henry said.

'Isn't that who you meant Maggie? Isn't that who Henry saw you with? Isn't that the shadow that always seems to be on your shoulder.'

Maggie became agitated and started to pace the room. 'I don't know who he is. I never asked his name. I just know he … follows me around sometimes. It got worse after Henry and I married. He even followed us when we left the plantation.'

'You're saying the man I saw you with was some kind of … ghost?' Henry said.

Maggie nodded. 'He's been around all my life. But … when I started to grow up it all got worse.'

Maggie didn't know what the spirit, or demon as I believed him to be, wanted. She felt harried by him though. It was like bad luck following her everywhere.

I questioned her more about the ritual she had taken part in earlier.

'It was to protect any children that Henry and I might have.'

'I figured out that much on my own. Protect them from what though?'

Maggie shook her head. 'I don't know. I thought it meant they would never be able to be *haunted* by this thing.'

'I have a feeling I know who will know more,' I said. 'Henry, are you willing to help Maggie through this? Before the day is out we may learn a lot more about her and the family.'

Henry took Maggie's hand. 'Yes. I'm still not sure what's happening but I'm willing to try and get answers if it means we will be able to live a normal life again.'

Maggie smiled at him and I saw hope in her eyes for the first time.

16

We found Big Momma in the garden. She was sitting at the table overlooking the lake, a fresh pot of tea was brewing and several cups and saucers had been laid out as though she were expecting us. Quietly we all joined her. I sat down opposite her, my back to the lake and Henry and Maggie sat either side.

'You need to tell the truth, Momma,' Maggie said taking her hand. 'This whole thing is ruining my life. I know I'm not insane now. Too many people have seen *It*.'

Big Momma was in the process of pouring tea into one of the cups. She stopped as Maggie spoke and put down the pot. Then she glanced back at the airship which almost completely blocked the view of the house from our position.

'Kat dear, is your friend planning to stay long?' asked Big Momma.

'We plan to stay as long as it takes. I decided this morning that I'm not leaving Pollitt Plantation until I solve this mystery. You want rid of us, then you tell me what all this is about.'

Big Momma sighed. She looked tired. Fragile. All of her vivacity had evaporated.

'I married Big Daddy very young,' she said. 'But I always loved him. Even when he didn't show me any emotion in return. He isn't a sentimental sort you know.'

I sat back in the chair, briefly wondering where Mother, Sally, Pepper and Martin were. But I pushed aside the thought that I hadn't seen any of them all day, reasoning that they had probably decided to go out on a trip.

'I fell pregnant almost immediately with you and Orlando, Maggie. Did I ever tell you that? Big Daddy and I are looking forward to the day when you make us proud grandparents too.'

'Momma ...' Maggie said. 'Please.'

'I was an orphan when I met Big Daddy. Left alone to fend for my young sister,' Big Momma continued. 'Alice is her name. And she came with me to the Plantation after we married. We came from simple folk. We didn't have slaves and Alice found them unnerving right from the start. But I hoped in time that she would get used to their ways, just as I would. I was of course determined to get used to everything here. I loved Pollitt Plantation right away. The sense of space, the history of the land and of Big Daddy's people, and I liked the slaves. There was something about being surrounded by people that made me feel safe. Cared for. Do you know what I mean? I didn't have to worry about anything anymore. It was a massive relief after the years of caring for sick parents and a younger sister.

'We settled into a quiet life on the plantation after the initial parties introduced me as Big Daddy's wife. Alice enjoyed those too. She was only sixteen at the time and it was all new and exciting for her too.

'After the first couple of months though, Alice started saying all kinds of crazy things about the house, about the slaves, about magic and superstition. She said she saw ghosts outside of the house. That the dead haunted the lands. I didn't believe any of it of course. She had always had an overactive imagination and so I just put it down to the huge changes in our life and tried to spend a little more time with her in the day when Big Daddy was out with the overseers taking care of business.

'But Alice wouldn't leave it be. Sometimes she woke in the night, screaming and crying, saying that someone had tried to get inside her room from the balcony outside.

'Soon the servants caught her terrors and they began to talk about evil spirits. Alice said she had seen a black figure walking the plantation at night. And the slaves began to get excited that some form of devil was on the land.

'Big Daddy and I didn't know what to do. Some of the slaves were calling her poor mad Miss Alice, while others were buying into the story. We even had a few of the girls try to run away. A situation that Big Daddy just couldn't tolerate. He had to do something about it. And so he asked around the Cajun quarter for someone who could help dispel our troubles and investigate if there was any basis to Alice's story. He reasoned that if he could prove it was imagination then Alice would settle down, forget this craziness and so would the slaves.

'A friend of Big Daddy's recommended getting in a preacher to sanctify the land. We decided that this was a good idea and so Big Daddy sent out one of the overseers to get the man they all seemed to recommend. His name was Derrin Callon, he was something of a new religion sort but we didn't care if he could disprove all the hocus-pocus that was causing such unrest. It was truly an unnerving time for me. And at the same time I also fell pregnant and was feeling sick and suffering a lot from the heat.

'I wasn't up and about the night that Callon arrived. I was lying in bed, feeling terribly sorry for myself and cursing the idea that I would have to suffer like this for many months to come, but Alice liked the man immediately and she came into my room to thank me for getting such efficient help. She felt sure that Callon would see away any of the spirits that might be lurking.

'The next day I was feeling better and so I went down to have a late breakfast and met the man for the first time.'

'He had yellow eyes,' Maggie said.

Big Momma nodded. 'He was a peculiar sort. Charming and charismatic. He reminded me more of a conjuror than a preacher. He wore expensive clothing, acted like a gentleman. Alice was quite taken with him. "With your permission," Callon said, "I would like to move into the house for a time. This way I can properly assess what is wrong here. It may take a few months. But I am certain you will see improvement all round."

'He said he "sensed" something. He made references and comments that fed Alice's phobias. But privately, when she wasn't around, he explained that this was all a ruse. He had to make her believe that she could trust him. That he wasn't there to disprove anything, but to find out the truth. Then he planned to show her that there were no ghosts and spirits. All of which he said he didn't really believe in. He said that Alice was suffering a malady of the mind. That sometimes white folks went like that when they were suddenly around the superstitions of the blacks. He said that Alice had probably heard some of the slaves talking their nonsense and it had somehow disturbed her peace of mind. In fact he told us exactly what we wanted to hear. What we ourselves thought was going on.

'We gave him a room that was situated at the end of the right wing, and Callon soon became part of our lives. He knew all about voodoo. Said he'd studied the slaves' religion and so knew how to deal with it all.

'A few weeks passed. Alice grew calm when Callon was in the house, but strange and confused whenever he left to go and take care of some business elsewhere. Sometimes he would be gone for a few days. And we noticed the difference in her at those times. It was always a relief when he returned. Alice became instantly calm. He was no trouble to have around either and made a charming addition to the household. All of the family and overseers liked and trusted him. He had that way with people. He could just put you right at ease.

'And Big Daddy was real happy too. He didn't want unsettled slaves. He didn't want to start having to beat sense into them. He's always been a gentle soul and never liked that kind of thing, saying that "kindness" was a better way to keep them in check. Callon's presence seemed to settle them down also and so his presence in our home became something we started to accept and take for granted.

'After a while things returned to normal. Alice was happy again. Sometimes she would get real shy around Callon and we began to think that she and him would probably marry at some point. We didn't know his origins and it never occurred to us to ask who his people were. He was certainly attentive and kind to Alice, and we didn't mind the idea of her marrying a preacher. There seemed nothing bad in the situation at all.

'Then Isaac approached Big Daddy out of the blue and asked him, "When is that … *thing* gonna leave here?" Big Daddy was taken aback by his head house slave talking to him so forward like that. He had always liked Isaac though. The slave worked hard and had never given him one jot of trouble. So he looked at him surprised and said, "Who are you talking about?"

'We were in the orangery and Isaac nodded out towards the doors. We looked out and saw Callon standing outside, looking in at us like he didn't even know who we were. "What's gotten into you Isaac?" Big Daddy said. You see by that time, Callon had pretty much become part of the family. We were completely comfortable with his presence and it never occurred to us to wonder how he had so easily become part of our lives like that. Or why.

'Isaac just shook his head. "You can't see it," he said. "But that *thing* ain't human." Well of course Big Daddy questioned him. But Isaac didn't make any more sense no matter what we asked. He just kept insisting that Callon was some kind of … devil. He called him a *kishi*. But when Big Daddy asked him to describe what that was, Isaac wouldn't.

'That night we heard the drums on the plantation for the first time but when the overseers searched the land they never found the instrument, nor the player. Every night, for a few hours, the drums beat. It became a source of frustration to the overseers that they couldn't find the culprit. They saw it as some kind of protest that the slaves were making and were suspicious of its meaning.

'About a week later, Alice came to me and said she was afraid for her life. I thought this was just because of the drums. They seemed to upset everyone but me. I liked them. They lulled me to sleep at night and strangely they made me feel safe.

'But Alice told me she had seen that dark spirit again. We had thought that all of this nonsense was now behind us. "I almost dropped my hand mirror," she said. When I asked her to describe what she saw, she said "Mister Callon … He was *in* my room. When I looked at him in the silver mirror he was the ghost I'd seen. When I looked at him directly he was Callon."

'Alice had tried to hide what she had seen from him

though. She asked him what he was doing in her room, he merely stared at her. Alice told me that she then began to feel drowsy. She likened the sensation to the excesses of wine on the occasions when she had been allowed to drink it with the family. She didn't feel in total control of herself, and she began to sway. At that moment, one of the servants knocked on the door to bring her some fresh linen.

'Alice says she jumped awake, and found herself lying back on the bed. Her skirt was raised up to her thighs and she thought she saw this black shadow disappear out through the open balcony door. She quickly straightened her dress and called in the girl. But she was shaken and afraid.

'Obviously I told Big Daddy immediately about the incident. He called Callon in and spoke to him, but of course he denied everything. He said he had been out riding at the time and the grooms confirmed his story. Big Daddy had no reason to disbelieve him. He said that Alice was probably dreaming the whole thing. She was, he thought, quite infatuated with Callon. Even so Big Daddy was concerned and a creeping suspicion was nagging at the back of his mind the whole time. He was worried about the slaves' dislike of Callon, and so he discussed the possibility of him leaving the plantation for a little while to see if Alice was better now.

'Of course Callon, being his usual amicable self, agreed and he packed his things and left the very next day.

'Isaac and the slaves seemed happier after that. I had seen a growing unrest among them, a kind of quiet disapproval that made me feel nervous and confused. We dropped back into the life we'd had before. Quiet, happy and, what's more the drums stopped at night which made me think that perhaps Callon had been the cause of them after all.

'Even so, Alice refused to sleep alone. She kept one of the slave girls in there with her at all times. She was acting oddly again but she didn't start on about seeing the ghost. Despite what we had thought she felt for Callon she seemed relieved he was out of the house. I began to think that she was going to get better after all. It would just take time. I listed out in my mind all that she had been through since our parents died, particularly the insecurity of our financial circumstances. All of this must have had some bearing on her state of mind. Especially when we were suddenly in the middle of nowhere, surrounded by slaves.

'A few weeks later Big Daddy told me he had to go away for a few days to take care of business in the port of New Orleans. Although the port and centre are in travelling distance of the Plantation, it was sometimes more convenient for him to stay there a night or two, rather than have a long ride in and out for the duration. Before my pregnancy I would go with him and we would eat at some of the cosmopolitan restaurants around the docks in the evening and while he worked in the day I would have fun shopping in the markets, with a team of slaves in tow to take home all of the lovely things I found. Of course this time, the doctor had told me I wasn't to travel. The heat had been getting to me a lot, and I'd only just started to feel less sick in the mornings. Besides, I didn't want to leave Alice alone. I was worried for her.

'The first night Big Daddy was away I heard the drums again, but they were faint, as though they were some distance away from the Plantation and especially the house. It was strange but I found them reassuring. Like they were playing to ward off evil. And as I drifted to sleep I felt safe and happy, like something good was trying to watch over me.

'In the middle of the night I woke up. I felt this strange pressure on my chest. Like something was on top of me, crushing me down into the bed. I cried out. The pressure lifted, and a blast of air whooshed out through the open balcony doors. It was hot, but I had thought I had closed the doors that night to keep out the mosquitoes. I got up and closed the doors thinking that I must have been mistaken.

'I vaguely remembered the sound of the drums as I had fallen asleep, but I even thought I had imagined that too.

'The next day I woke feeling tired and drained as if I hadn't slept at all, and yet even though I had awakened in the night to the strange dream, and the feeling that someone was in the room with me, I had rapidly fallen back into a drug-like sleep.

'At breakfast Isaac served me as usual, but I found him looking at me intently on more than one occasion. Eventually I sent him away. His scrutiny was making me feel uncomfortable and I was determined to tell Big Daddy about his odd behaviour when he returned home.

'That night I was tortured with strange dreams once more. There was that pressure feeling again. I struggled to wake, but I couldn't open my eyes. The weight made me feel sick again and the next day, when my servant came in to help me dress she found me lying across the bed in a dead faint.

'Isaac sent for the doctor immediately, and when Big Daddy returned the doctor told him I was suffering from some malady induced by the pregnancy and heat. There were even fears that I had contracted some sort of swamp fever, that might have been passed to me from the incessant assault of mosquitoes that plagued us so much at that time of year.

'But with Big Daddy back, I began to sleep better again and I soon recovered from whatever had been ailing me.

'Of course the same couldn't be said for Alice. She got sick. So much so that the doctor recommended we send her away for her own health's sake. Whatever illness had touched me, began to eat away at her and she suffered more and more with her delusions.

'When we found out that she was carrying a child, Big Daddy and I made the decision to send her away immediately before the scandal brought shame on the Plantation. She couldn't tell us who the father was, denying that it was even possible. Her lying angered Big Daddy and it made him more determined not to have her around anymore. We suspected that the father was Callon, but part of me didn't want to believe that a preacher could take advantage of a young innocent girl like that. But he was the only man that had been given freedom in our home.

'The day we sent her away Alice seemed relieved to go. She let the servants pack her things with barely a murmur and she left with a small chaperone of slaves and men to take her all the way to the hospital in Mississippi.

'A few weeks later we received word that Alice had lost the baby. The journey had been too arduous for her weakened state. I felt just awful about it, especially in my condition. It had to be for the best though: she would have been ruined. When we learnt that the experience had completely driven the last bit of sanity from her mind I felt terrible guilt. As though I had failed to protect her.

'Obviously Big Daddy sent money to secure the best care for her, and we received six-monthly reports, but Alice never recovered from her experience and isn't likely too either.

'I had Big Daddy question all of the white men on the plantation again. We knew that one of them had to have been responsible for Alice's condition. Maybe he had even disguised himself as some spirit. And I reminded Big Daddy about the story she had told, of being drowsy, of Callon and of waking up with her clothing pulled up. Callon had been gone a while before the pregnancy became known though, and we hadn't heard from him since.'

Big Momma paused in her story and she looked from Maggie, to Henry and then to me.

'I'll get to the point,' she said quietly. 'Some months later I gave birth to my babies. When Orlando came out, Big Daddy came rushing in to hold his son. Nanny Simone held out the baby to him and at that point he opened his eyes and yelled with lungs that a wolf would have been proud of. Big Daddy smiled down at the baby and then he froze. I've never seen a man of ruddy complexion go so instantly white. "He's not mine …" he declared and he refused to take him. Then he stormed from the room.

'I began to cry. All the pain I'd gone through, and now my husband, to whom I'd been completely faithful, was denying his own child. I couldn't believe it. Well with every tear the pains began again, and soon Nanny Simone realised what was happening. "Why you is having another one, Miss Cherie," she said. And indeed I was. A few moments later Maggie was born, and Nanny Simone rushed out to show her to Big Daddy.

'Soon after that he came back in. He refused to look at Orlando, and when Nanny Simone passed him to me to press to my breast, I suddenly learnt why. Orlando's eyes were yellow and I had only ever seen one person with such a strange feature. Callon. I gasped and cried, pushing him away as I begged to see my baby girl. Nanny Simone took the baby back. "Don't worry none," she said. "We will make sure he gets milk from one of the other suckling mothers on the plantation." I knew she meant one of the slave girls but I didn't care. To me Orlando looked like something spawned of the devil.

'Nanny Simone passed you to me, Maggie, reassuring me like she did Big Daddy. Then she took Big Daddy aside and said he needed to go and see Isaac. That he could explain what had happened right enough. You see, they had seen this sort of thing before and Nanny Simone remembered the tales her parents told of the *kishi*. Who, she explained, was a demon that impersonated a human.

'Big Daddy went away just like she said. Then he came back to me. He held me and told me how he knew this wasn't my fault. Isaac had told him who the demon was, and how he had managed to do this.'

'Callon had been the spirit that you felt crushing you,' I said.

'Yes Miss Kat. And the whole thing wasn't over yet.'

Maggie hugged her mother. 'This must have been so awful for you. And I remember, Orlando wasn't kept in the nursery with Amelia and I. But doesn't this mean … that Callon was my father too?'

'Oh no, Miss Maggie,' said a deep voice from behind us. 'Orlando was the only brood of that demon.'

We all looked around to see Isaac standing by the door into the house. His face was serious as he walked over and joined us at the table. He sat down with us just like he was a member of the family and I knew that another important story was about to be told.

17

'Orlando was the *only* brood of that demon,' repeated Isaac, looking into each of our eyes in turn. 'He used Big Momma's already working womb to create another life is all. He failed with Miss Alice you see. The human body wasn't made to work with a demon that way. Demons can only birth dead babies. But the *kishi*, he had realised a way around it. He gave Big Momma another baby. This baby gained life because of you, Miss Maggie, because you were in there keeping his coldness warm.'

'This is all so awful,' Maggie said. 'I love my brother. He hasn't got an evil bone in his body. None of this can be his fault.'

'That's true,' said Isaac. 'He is half-human after all and …'

'And what?' I asked, but Isaac let the sentence hang there.

'Orlando is a sweet innocent,' Big Momma said again. 'But he wasn't always that way. He …'

Big Momma glanced at Maggie and tears sprang into her eyes. 'He tried to drown his sister. We had to do something

164

after that.'

'Momma, what do you mean? Orlando never hurt me.'

'It was Miss Amelia he tried to drown,' said Isaac quietly. 'Out there in that lake.'

'We found her body floating out there,' Big Momma continued. 'She was all but dead. If it hadn't been for Isaac's quick thinking. He threw himself into the water, dragged her out and somehow managed to shake the water from her lungs. She woke up, coughing and spluttering, and she told us who'd done it. "It was Dando, Momma," she told me.'

'Dando?' I said. 'Oh my goodness.' Suddenly I knew who the child was that I had been seeing. It was Orlando of course. It all made sense. Why hadn't I realised it sooner?

'Yes, that was the name I had for him because I couldn't pronounce Orlando properly. It sort of stuck after that. Though we never call him by that name anymore,' said Maggie. 'But I don't believe Orlando hurt Amelia. You need to understand something, Momma. Although you all tried to keep us apart, Orlando and I shared the same womb. We also shared feelings. He never did this Momma, I'm sure of it.'

'Maggie is right,' I said. 'I don't think Orlando hurt anyone.'

'If it wasn't him,' asked Henry. 'Then who did?'

What Big Momma didn't know was that Isaac and Big Daddy had come to an agreement the night that Orlando was born.

'You wasn't to know,' Isaac had said to Big Daddy all those years ago, 'but those things are tricksy. They hide in plain sight. Why that creature was trying to get access to Miss Alice all along. Once you let him in he had the right to come and go as he pleased.'

'But what can we do?' asked Big Daddy. 'There has to be somethin'. Maybe we need to send for a real priest, get this place exorcised.'

'That won't work,' Isaac told him. 'This is old evil and old evil needs old magic. I can help you but I need something in return.'

Big Daddy had listened to Isaac's proposal. The slave told him that he was a voodoo priest, that he could lift the curse, but it required a sacrifice on Big Daddy's part.

'I can't justify killin' someone to rid us of this thing,' Big Daddy said.

'This ain't about death. It's about freedom,' said Isaac. 'Our freedom. Big Daddy you always been a fair and jus' masser. We have nothing to complain about. We have homes, we have food. You don't condone beating or the abusing of our women folk. Otherwise, I'd more'n likely jus' sit back and let this thing eat you alive. But we seen good in you and we all love Miss Cherie. She don't deserve none of this badness in her life. But let me tell you this. If I could *give* you this magic I would. But magic don't work unless you is prepared to pay a price that means something to you. A sacrifice.'

'You want your freedom?' Big Daddy had said. 'That isn't a sacrifice for me and I willingly give it you if you can do what you say.'

'I want to be your *employee*, just like your white

overseers are. Big Daddy, I'm happy to work for you until my body decays and gives out, but I wanna do this as a free man. But I also want freedom for everyone else on this plantation. That is a sacrifice I think be fitting.'

Big Daddy took some time to think about this. He waited five years to finalise the agreement, even though in principle he had always agreed. He just had to take his time to do this thing, step by step. And by taking that long it proved how difficult it was for Big Daddy to let go of his possession of them all. After all it went against everything he was used to. During those years the drums played every night. The slaves feared the *kishi* and they wanted to keep their own pregnant women safe from its evil influence.

Isaac explained that all of them sacrificed something dear to them in order for it to work. It didn't matter, you see, how big or small the forfeit was, all that mattered was that the giving was hard, and heart-felt.

The magic worked. Little by little it weakened Callon and protected the slaves as well as the white folks who lived in the house.

But the demon still walked the halls of the Plantation at night and Big Momma, as she had now started to be called, saw him sometimes standing by the lake. He would beckon to her. Try to get her to come out to him. But she always resisted. And when she found herself pregnant with her second child, Big Daddy never left her side until the day Amelia was born.

It was Amelia's attempted murder that was the last straw for Big Daddy. That night he went to Isaac, a wad of papers in his hand, each containing the name of one of the slaves. He freed the entire plantation in one go, just like Isaac wanted him to and he swore an allegiance to always protect the land where they all lived from the Darkness that would try in many forms to take men's souls.

After that the rituals began. Some of which Big Momma was a part of, some of which she wasn't, but always Big Daddy was there and he'd fall into a trance state which would allow him to channel the energy out up into the sky and then to send the light out into all the dark places for miles around. He was a conduit of sorts, because Isaac knew he had a pure soul.

'I had to be present the night they took Orlando,' Big Momma said. 'The sacrifice had to come from me as well. And believe me there's no bigger price to pay than a mother's fear for her own children. Orlando was my child and a part of me. I loved him and I thought he was going to be the forfeit. And I was trying to come to terms with the idea that my son was gonna die even as they lay his terrified body on an altar.'

Tears ran down Big Momma's cheeks as she recalled that awful day. 'But we couldn't let Orlando be, no matter what the price. What if he tried to kill Amelia again, or even Maggie? It was too much of a risk.'

'What did the ritual really do?' I asked Isaac.

'We did what we thought was best ...' the old servant said, bowing his head.

He described a similar ritual to the one that I had witnessed earlier that day. This of course with Orlando as the focus, tied down – he said – for his own safety. But I could see why Big Momma would have been afraid. Under normal circumstances if I had come across this scenario I'd have been in there trying to save a boy I thought was in danger.

'I saw Callon standing on the outskirts, looking in at me,' Big Momma said. 'He was trying to stop us, but Isaac's magic has real power. Outside of that circle stood all the forces of evil and it couldn't touch us while we remained inside.'

'It's light,' I said and they all looked at me surprised that I understood it. 'Light always disperses the dark. It's the one thing the Darkness really fears.'

'Yes, Miss Kat,' said Isaac, 'but we didn't count on Callon outwitting us.'

Big Momma shook her head as though she wanted Isaac to stop telling his story but he continued on as though the burden he had been carrying all these years could finally be relieved.

'Callon brought Miss Amelia and Miss Maggie out of the house and down to the circle. As we began to separate the demon side from Orlando, planning to trap it in the world that only the dead can live, Miss Amelia began to cry.

'Well, Big Momma was all ready to run out there to save her little girls, but I knowed it was a demon trick. I had both those little 'uns tucked away safe being guarded by someone I trusted and hidden by a circle of protection. Those things that looked like them were something he'd brought out from hell to fool us with.'

Big Momma was sobbing openly now as she recalled

what must have been the most traumatic night of her life.

'We were safe, Orlando was safe,' Isaac continued, 'and I knew the girls were too. But Big Momma took it bad. We had to hold her down, and while I was distracted, trying to make sure she did all she was supposed to or the magic wouldn't work, Orlando wriggled his way free of the bonds that held him down. He was half-way across the clearing to Callon when we realised.

'Several of the congregation ran after the boy. All the time I'm yelling that they ain't to break the circle, no matter what. I didn't want those demon children getting in there, there was no saying what might o' happened.

'Orlando reached the edge though, and the thing that I'd most hoped for happened. His demon side couldn't cross over. He couldn't leave no matter how much that *kishi* reached for him.

'The demon began to consume the things that looked like Miss Amelia and Miss Maggie. Biting chunks out of their small arms just like they was fruit he'd picked off a tree. Big Momma began a yellin' an' a cryin' She was losing her mind but I needed her to stay focused. To help us take the bad right out of the boy. I slapped her face, made her kneel before the altar, as some of the group caught hold of Orlando and brought him back where we needed him. "You got to listen now," I say to Big Momma, all quiet like to keep her calm. "This be your sacrifice. You have to let the girls go, if you wanna save Orlando. And believe me his human side don' deserve to be tied to that thing its whole life."

'Big Momma fell into a shocked stillness, but I took this as her acceptance of the potential sacrifice. She didn't know that I'd have never risked the life of those two girls, not for all the world, and so her heart pain was real and so was her love for Orlando. She was torn apart by the choice she was having to make. But it was what the magic needed to work.

'The time was getting on, we only had a small slot when the midday sun was at its strongest, and so I began the ritual.'

Isaac described how the spell they cast could separate evil from a man's soul, and how they used this on the boy to remove the demon side of his nature.

'Afterwards Orlando was unhurt,' Isaac said, 'and now he was a good child. An angel. He was so perfect that even Big Momma and Big Daddy could done bring him completely into their family.'

'But his eyes …' Big Momma said.

'His eyes didn't change. Not like Big Daddy's had done. This ain't no science an' I can't predict or control the result like I'd want to,' Isaac said. 'Big Daddy, he still couldn't love the boy the same. But Big Momma, she always loved him, demon side an' all.'

'I assume that wasn't the end of it of course?' I said. 'Callon was still there.'

Isaac shook his head. 'No. The demon jus' dis'pear'd as well. We was alert for a long time but after that the sightings jus' dried up.

'Then, as Miss Maggie grew, Nanny Simone reported that the little girl was "seeing" things and having strange dreams and the like. I persuaded Simone to convince her it was all imagination, and also to plant the idea that Miss Maggie wasn't to look directly at any wayward spirit she thought she saw. Simone told her tales about her poor mad Aunt Alice and it proved to be enough for quite some time. The girl refused to recognize Callon. You see when they knows you see them, they gains power.'

'But I was aware he was there,' Maggie said. 'I didn't know who it was. But I always could feel him nearby.'

'Then she got a fright one night. That thing decided to force her to look at him. But he weren't no handsome man, no more, that reach the heart of some poor weak-minded female. Something we'd taken from Orlando had also been pulled from him too. He was powerless unless he got another girl with his chile.

'We knowed he was coming after Miss Maggie after that though, and now she wed … he's after attaching himself to any baby that might spring up in her belly. Just as he did with Big Momma.'

'Well, there's not much chance of that at the moment,' Maggie said. She glanced over at Henry who had remained quiet all the time but had been listening intently to the whole story.

'Maggie, this thing isn't going to get you,' Henry said. 'You're my wife and I've sworn to protect you. Now I know the whole story, the strange things I've seen around here make sense.'

'I'd never betray you, Henry. But you see now why it was so difficult to explain?'

He took her hand and I suddenly knew that their relationship, now that the truth was told, was going to survive this.

'Today, when I took part in one of Isaac's rituals,' Maggie said to me. 'I was trying to make sure our future children would be safe.'

'I know,' I said. 'One thing that does confuse me though Isaac. How come this thing didn't seduce Maggie? And why has Amelia remained safe so far? I assume that all of her children are … human?'

'After she *saw* the thing, I had Maggie sent away to a boarding school in South Carolina,' said Big Momma. 'I couldn't risk him messing with either of the girls and so when Amelia was old enough, she was sent also. Even so, Callon seems to have a dislike for Amelia and as far as we know has never attempted to interfere with her.'

'Plus,' said Isaac. 'Miss Maggie shared a womb with his chile'. She be more receptive than most to the demon. She always been sweet-natured, but strong. She ain't tainted by it, but she be *close* to it. If you get my meaning? Whereas Miss Amelia don't have a spiritual bone in her body.'

'And,' said Big Momma. 'Big Daddy and I never allowed Maggie and Amelia to come home for long periods during those years. When they did they always slept in the same room as one of the servants. We even used to travel over and collect them during the break times. Taking trips and family holidays away from the Plantation. When Maggie finally came home for good though, we felt Callon sniffing around again.

'Although we didn't wholly approve of the wedding, when Maggie eloped with Henry we realised it was something of a mixed blessing. Parents always want their children to stay home and although it made me real sad, I wanted the girls to be happy and settled away from here.'

There was a pause and we all sat quietly, thinking over what had been revealed.

'This is quite a story,' I said eventually. 'I need to share with my colleagues as soon as possible. Does anyone know where Pepper and Martin have gone? I've been looking around for them all day.'

'Why I thought you knew,' Big Momma said surprised. 'Mr Crewe and Mr Pepper took your Momma and Miss Sally to the train today to send them home. I must admit I encouraged it. I was worried about Miss Sally's safety all the time. In fact I think that all the young women should leave, you and Maggie too, as soon as possible until we figure out what to do here.'

'I can't do that, Big Momma. I have to see this through. Somehow we are going to destroy this creature for good. You see, this is my job. I do this kind of thing all the time.'

Isaac smiled at me across the table. 'You see, Big Momma, I tol' you she was the one.'

At that moment a horse-drawn carriage clattered up the drive, and Pepper and Martin disembarked. I waved to them.

'Thank goodness!' I said. Then I turned back to the others still sitting at the table. 'I will find you all later. Until then we still have another mystery to solve, and I know it is somehow linked, I just don't know yet how much.'

I stood and headed over to meet Pepper and Martin, leaving Big Momma, Henry, Maggie and Isaac staring after me.

18

After explaining the lengthy story to Pepper and Martin, and hearing how they had persuaded Mother to take Sally home – for which I was very grateful – we returned once more to the landing in the left wing of the house. There was still one big hole left in this mystery that needed to be filled. Where had Callon come from in the first place? Why had he chosen Pollitt Plantation to victimise? And why didn't he leave now that the family and the slaves were aware of him? After all, wouldn't it be easier for him to trick some other poor unsuspecting family into allowing him into their homes?

'What we know so far,' Martin summarised, 'is that Callon couldn't enter the house at all until the family invited him to stay here.'

'That's right,' I said. 'After that he seemed to be able to go wherever he pleased.'

'There's some link with the house, the land, and I

think this room you've seen Dando in. Who, we can guess, is probably the demon half of Orlando, trapped in some form of hell that takes the shape of the room,' Martin said.

'Even so, Big Momma insists there was never an extra room down here,' Pepper said. 'Yet you're drawn there constantly, Kat. Perhaps Pollitt Plantation has history, maybe one of Big Daddy's ancestors hid a room behind this wall.'

'How do you come to that conclusion?' I asked.

'Because while we were driving back from New Orleans I studied the layout of the house. From the road I could see that the left wing had 12 windows all along the second floor. When we got here, I counted 11 windows and 11 doors that open onto the balcony on the right wing. I also noticed that there is a whole room's length on the end of the house that has neither window nor door.'

It was true that the length of the landing extended beyond the final door – Pepper's room – all the way to the end. There could and should be a room there. But I was certain that Big Momma didn't know about it if there was. Perhaps Big Daddy did though.

'No time to ask him,' Martin said as he removed a saw and a hammer from the large bag he was carrying. 'I'm going to knock a hole through this wall and find out what's hidden here. Pepper, I'll need you to block anyone who tries to stop me.'

'I'm not sure that we should do this without permission,' I said.

Martin frowned. 'Do you think it's likely that we will be given permission?'

I thought for a moment then shook my head. 'No. I think they will probably ask us to leave.'

'Then … we have nothing to lose by being brutal,' said Martin. 'It's all for their own good anyway.'

I wasn't completely comfortable with the idea of the destruction, but I did agree with his sentiment at least, that this was for the greater good.

I was surprised to see him using such basic tools, until I noticed a SunPan on the top of the saw. I was soon to learn that the saw had a line of laser light that poured from the tip and out along the jagged edges, that otherwise appeared to be completely normal. Martin walked along the wall, tapping gently with the handle of the hammer. The walls all seemed solid until he was halfway along and the tone of the tap changed. He glanced over his shoulder at me, then swung the hammer as hard as he could against what he believed to be the concealed entrance.

As he worked, I went back to my room and changed back into my dry breeches. This time I added my weapons belt, from which hung my clockwork crossbow: a reliable weapon because it only needed winding up to be fully operational; a round-barrel cartridge that contained a selection of silver tipped arrows that would load and fire from the crossbow in rapid succession; my Perkins-Armley, ready loaded with darts and at the last moment I placed the silver and diamond-shard knife in the sheath in my boot, finishing my ensemble.

By the time I returned to the landing I found that the hammering and sawing had drawn some of the household staff. One of the servants, on seeing what we were doing, rushed away to tell Big Daddy. Within a few moments Big Daddy came bounding up the stairs.

'What the devil's going on up here?'

Martin ignored him and swung the hammer as hard as he could. The smash echoed down the landing with a hollow thump and I knew he was almost through to the secret room.

'Stop it!' Big Daddy cried.

Isaac and Big Momma hurried upstairs to see what all the commotion was.

'What's happening?' asked Big Momma when she saw the mess. Her eyes swept over my outfit and weapons and she took a step back as though the sight of me was intimidating, which I suppose it must have been.

Martin was now using the laser saw, and it was burning a door-shaped hole in the wall. Realising that yelling was not doing any good, Big Daddy tried to snatch the tool from Martin's hand, but Pepper blocked him as he had promised he would.

He spun the big man around using his considerable weight to propel him back down the corridor. It was somewhat comedic but I didn't laugh because Big Momma and Isaac took it all so seriously. As Big Daddy stumbled into the wall opposite he went into a rage like none of us had ever seen. It took Isaac and two of the other male servants to hold him back.

'Big Daddy,' Isaac said. 'It's time this was done. You can' let this go on no longer.'

Big Daddy crumpled, holding his chest as though he were in tremendous pain as Martin resumed his sawing. With every cut made to the wall he cried out in agony and rolled around on the floor.

'What's wrong with him?' Big Momma said. Up until that moment she had been rooted to the spot as though her feet were caught in mud. Now she fell to her knees beside Big Daddy and held him tight even as he struggled against her.

'Go on,' said Isaac to Martin. 'This has to be done.'

Martin studied Isaac for a moment and I realised that we were on the right track, that there really was something to find behind that wall, and that it had been hidden there for some time. Isaac, I realised, was as curious as the rest of us as to what that was. I suspected that he'd had suspicions for a long time that there was a room hidden here, but had been unable to act on it.

The first panel of wood tumbled inwards and Martin called for a light. Milly looked over at Isaac, and when he nodded to confirm she should obey, she hurried away to the nearest bedroom, returning moments later with a lit lantern. It seemed that everyone wanted to know what we had found.

Big Daddy was quiet now, though he sobbed against Big Momma like a child who had fallen down and couldn't get back up again. He seemed terrified by the whole ordeal but his eyes were fixed upon the opening as Martin smashed through a little more, and a bead of sweat burst out on the big man's forehead, as though it were he that was exerted and not my friend.

I took the light from Milly and walked towards the hole.

'Is this what you saw, Kat?' Pepper asked as the three of us looked through the newly-opened doorway.

The light from the lamp cast a dreary glow into the space. In the centre of the room I saw the same huge bed, sheets rotted and moth-eaten, while a thick layer of dust covered the floor. The room was set much as it had been, except that it was old and deteriorated and stank of stale air and decay.

'Yes. It's the same room, though I saw it fresh and clean. This is years of rot.'

'Get more lamps,' ordered Pepper, and a few of the servants went to the task.

I stepped over the threshold, felt that rush of vacuum sound, but knew that this time I wasn't crossing some strange dimensional doorway, the sensation was merely because this room had been blocked off for so long from the fresh and natural circulation of air and sound. I turned around, taking in the chest of drawers, the rocking chair in the corner … all the things I had seen in there before. There were shutters and dust-heavy curtains placed over where the window and doorway to the balcony should have been.

I walked towards the bed. In my mind's eye I saw once again the lonely little boy sitting amongst the cushions and crying.

Pepper and Martin had followed me inside, both carrying lamps and the room slowly filled with light.

'What is this place?' Big Momma said from the doorway.

'I think you will have to ask Big Daddy,' I said.

Big Momma turned to look at her husband, who was still, I assumed, on the floor in the corridor.

'What's going on?' she asked him. 'How long has this room been here?'

I heard movement outside as the old man staggered to

his feet. I left Pepper and Martin to look around, I already knew the place well enough, and I went outside into the corridor to see Isaac and another manservant supporting Big Daddy.

'Take me to my room,' Big Daddy said.

They helped him limp away, back to the left wing where he and Big Momma slept. Big Momma stayed and she stared into the room with a look of bemusement and anxiety. She had good reason to be feeling both of these emotions too. Her hand absently picked at the splinters of wood around the opening. This room held the answers to the mystery that had been haunting this family for years.

'I found something,' said Martin behind me.

'What is it?' I asked.

Martin turned holding something in his hand. He had found it in one of the drawers of the dresser. 'It's a book. A journal. By someone called Dando ...'

'Dando?' said Big Momma. 'But that's not possible. My son was never in this room ...'

Martin carefully flicked through the book, the paper was old and brittle, and then looked up at Big Momma. 'It says Orlando Pollitt III in the back.'

'But ... but that's Big Daddy,' Big Momma said. 'It's a family tradition to name the first born son Orlando. Our son is the fourth.'

'Big Daddy is also called Orlando?' I said. 'And he was also known as Dando? This all getting rather confusing.'

'Well I wasn't expecting that,' Martin said. 'This was Big Daddy's room?'

19

'There was a young boy in the room,' I said. 'As well as Callon of course. This child told me he was being punished because he tried to drown his sister.'

Isaac was in the dining room, placing the highly polished silver onto the table for supper as though nothing had happened. I had tried to talk to Big Daddy but he had a servant posted by his door who wouldn't let anyone inside. Big Daddy was 'sick', he said. 'An' Big Momma tol' me no one was to disturb him.'

'I thought I had this whole thing figured out,' I said. 'I thought the boy was Orlando, Maggie's twin brother, not Orlando Senior – Big Daddy. I didn't see that coming.'

Isaac nodded and moved onto the next place setting.

'So, what I'm asking is … what do you know about this?'

'Know? I don't *know* anything, Miss Kat. I just had suspicions is all. I was young when Big Daddy was born but

I remember there being something about his eyes. Like they was yellow, like a cat's. At the time I worked the Plantation, not the house. I never seen nothin' nor been up here until after the last house manager disappear. He was my father, and had the gift too.'

'What gift?'

'We natural priests, Miss Kat, jus' as you is a natural seer and a demon-killer. Yes, I knowed that was what you was the minute you arrive here.'

'So, your father was a priest. Like you, and I assume your ancestors …?'

Isaac nodded. This information was predictable but what he said next wasn't.

'Big Daddy's father was the original *kishi*. I knowed that much. But this all raises questions as to what really happened to my own daddy.'

'What do you mean?'

Isaac stopped working and turned his sincere brown eyes to me. 'Miss Kat, I is about to tell you something I ain't never told no one. And I'm not even sure what happened myself.'

'Let's go outside,' I suggested.

Isaac called in another of the servants to take over setting the table, and he followed me out through the drawing room and onto the lawn. It was full dark now, but as usual the oil lamps were lit and we walked down the path to the lake and sat down at the table to talk.

Isaac lit the lamp in the centre of the table. I think this

was because he wanted me to see the honesty in his eyes as he told his story. Then he revealed to me what he believed to have happened all those years ago.

'I was fourteen at the time. My daddy was working up in the big house, having gained the trust of the Pollitts the night that the lady o' the house gave birth to two chil'ren. My daddy come home all agitated the night they was born and he say they is something wrong with one of the babes. My momma had jus' had a baby and she was to suckle this other chile too. Masser Pollitt he didn't want that boy to latch on to his wife's teat, even though we had no idea why. He had no trouble with the girl though, she was his pride and joy. But he was being all strange-like about the son. He called him Orlando though, as was the tradition on the family. All the first born boys were given this name and his daughter he named Susanna.

'Well my momma suckled that chile up at the house, but I never see him. Sometimes though she talk to my daddy about his eyes, saying that he look nothing like Masser Pollitt, but I paid it no mind, as I knowed Miss Lacey Pollitt wouldn't have been nowhere else: not a lady like that.

'Miss Lacey though, she was a sweet thing and she love that boy all the same, in spite of him being different. But when he was five, he and Miss Suzanna was found in the lake. I heard tell that young Misser Orlando was holding her head under the water and laughing like a devil from hell.

'The next day though, I was working in the garden. Cutting down the grass to keep Miss Lacey's lawn nice and I seen young Masser Orlando playing outside with Miss

Suzanna. He just like any little boy, and his eyes, they blue. I don't know why he even talked of as strange.

'What I didn't realise at the time was, Masser Pollitt had asked to see my daddy and the same deal, the same offer was given to him as I later gave Big Daddy. Masser Pollitt had to pay a price, a sacrifice, and the slaves had to be freed and he had agreed right enough.

'My daddy performed the ritual somewhere in the house although I didn't know where this took place, in those days there was no open congregation like we have now, we'd have been shot for witchcraft. The boy was cured, he was every bit a Pollitt now and no demon blood tainted his soul. But Masser Pollitt went back on his promise. He wasn't freeing no one, not now that he had his son back. What kind of inheritance would a Plantation be without its slaves after all?

'My daddy he took to cursing the Masser, which was how I learned of what had happened. After that he began to share his secrets with me, passing on years of knowledge in a single day by a ritual he made me take part in. My momma was afeared though. She knew no good would come of my daddy putting a hex on the Pollitts – but Masser Pollitt made his agreement and didn't pay the price. An' some forfeit had to be given for that. "But I ain't cursing him, don't you see?" my daddy said. "He brung this on hisself."

'My momma pleaded with my daddy to ask the Masser again to pay the price. "The boy has to be turned back," my daddy said. "The magic can't be cheated. There will be circumstances of the worse kind." But he agreed to go and

185

talk to Pollitt one last time that night when he served him his brandy in the study. "After that," he tol' us. "I won't be responsible for what is gonna happen."

'My daddy never came back that night. And we never saw him again. But in the middle of the night I woke up, scared and shaking. I knowed something had happened to him, and I knowed that I was now the priest of the congregation.

'The next day my momma was crying and holding my little sister. She said she knowed my daddy was dead, but no body was ever brought down from the house. Which was usually the way when a wayward slave was punished in those days. His body, dead or alive would be shown to us all as an example.

'O' course Masser Pollitt made out that my daddy had run away and beatings of some of the more surly among us began until he was sure we was all cowed. After that I was asked to go work in the big house, taking on my daddy's serving role. I think this was because the Masser wanted to keep an eye on me. But I kept all I knowed to myself.

'Even though my daddy had said there would be consequences, nothing happened at the big house. Masser Pollitt's son Orlando grew up fine and so did Miss Suzanna, and then when she entered her thirteenth year all kinds of strange things started to happen. Miss Suzanna went plum crazy with all the fear and scares that old ghost gave her. And Miss Lacey and Masser Pollitt married her off before she was even fifteen. After that, that old ghost done disappear again.

'Young Misser Orlando though, he was a good man. He grew up strong and tall and kind. When the Masser died, his old heart giving out one day, things on the plantation changed overnight. Misser Orlando didn't like no beatings. He talked nicely to us all and we grew to love him and want to stay and work on Pollitt Plantation as we knew no other place was ever going to be this nice for us. It was like he was trying to make up for what his daddy had done.

'As you know the rest there ain't no point in me continuing,' Isaac finished.

'Yes. When Orlando – Big Daddy – married Big Momma, the whole thing started again with Miss Alice.'

'There's a curse on this place,' said Isaac looking back at the house. 'And I don't know how to lift it. The price wasn't paid for Big Daddy's soul, and even though he saved his own son, and did pay, there's still a reckoning to be made.'

I left Isaac and went back into the house. I had no idea what I was going to do. Pollitt Plantation was being haunted by Callon. He would continue to stalk the Pollitt females, but where had he come from in the first place? Isaac had said Big Daddy's father was the *kishi*, but did he mean Master Pollitt, or did he mean Callon? And if Master Pollitt was already a demon, then why would he have the demon-side removed from his son?

None of it made sense. Nor did the fact that I could feel that the demon soul of Big Daddy, still in its child form, was trapped somehow between here and the next dimension. It was in a kind of limbo. And, if Dando was the demon-side of Big Daddy, he hadn't seemed that demonic to me. He was just like any ordinary child, with the exception of his strange eye colour.

'Perhaps it is limbo,' Martin said when I caught up with him and Pepper in the drawing room. 'I mean, perhaps that is the forfeit for not paying?'

The family was conspicuous by its absence. Amelia and Michel Beaugard had left that morning with their sons, but Maggie, Henry and Big Momma were also nowhere around.

'Certainly the hauntings are connected,' said Pepper. 'But what punishment is there in the demon half of Big Daddy being caught in limbo? It can't hurt anyone. Nor can it rejoin with Big Daddy, who to all intents and purposes has lived a good life and doesn't deserve such an evil end anyway.'

I was convinced that Big Daddy knew something. He had been afraid when we broke into the concealed room, and he had seemed to experience physical pain. Whether this was because he remembered the pain and trauma of the separation I didn't know.

'We need to speak to him,' I said. 'He needs to know the truth.'

'Agreed. But maybe Big Momma should be brought into this first. She might help us approach him,' Henry said from the doorway.

I turned around to see my brother and his wife Maggie.

'My daddy has a right to know what happened to him. And so does Orlando,' Maggie said.

It was then that it occurred to me to wonder where Orlando was. I hadn't seen him since our ride that morning. There had been so much going on, that I hadn't given him more than a cursory thought, and then only when his name had cropped up in the context of the stories that had been told.

'This has been a long day,' I said. 'Maybe we should sleep on it. But has anyone seen Orlando at all since this morning?'

20

I found my nightdress laid out on the bed and Milly running a bath for me as I entered my room. I was still in my breeches, having totally forgotten to change and remove my guns, but no one had said a word, or expressed any view that this wasn't normal. Not even my brother who, now that he knew his wife hadn't betrayed him, was being surprisingly accepting of the weirdness of the situation.

I thanked Milly and as she left, slipped gratefully out of my clothes and into the warm water. As I washed away the grime of the day, rinsing my hair, and lathering it with scented soap, I mulled over everything that had happened trying to make those elusive puzzle pieces fit in place.

Master Pollitt, Big Daddy's father, had started all this but it still seemed to me that the only people who had suffered were Big Daddy and his family. It hardly seemed fair. But that was the way of demons and unpaid-for magic. It never went how you expected.

I still couldn't understand who or what Callon was either. He was, presumably, the real father of both Big Daddy and Orlando. A tangled web if ever there was one … Which meant that somehow Maggie Pollitt did have demon blood in her, but it was inactive because … wait … Big Daddy had the demon-side ripped from him. But Maggie …

No. I shook my head. The thought was too ridiculous. Maggie was completely human and always had been, because Big Daddy was human when he married Big Momma and Maggie was conceived. It was only Orlando who had been fathered by Callon when Big Momma was already pregnant.

I sighed. This was all so complex and confusing. There was still so much information to assimilate but my head hurt from it all and I felt weary.

I felt guilty about the mindless destruction at the end of the landing. The hole had been a gaping dark maw in the dull gaslight as I had come onto the landing. It had seemed to stare at me accusingly. And other than finding Dando's journal – which told us nothing as it merely contained the scribbled drawings of a child – and the revelation that Big Daddy had once been the nephilim child, we had gained nothing by opening up the room. After all, what Isaac had told me since about his own father was something that I might have learnt anyway. All we had proved was that there was a room hidden behind the wall.

So – I had seen it: the room was real. So what! My revelation of this part of the mystery had only served to hurt a lot of people and I couldn't help feeling bad about that.

We had now outstayed our welcome at Pollitt Plantation, and I was certain that Mother would have plenty to say once she heard about it. I was only relieved that she and Sally were absent and now on their way home to New York. At least they were safe and could not be manipulated by Callon. In fact, I doubted that any of us could now that we knew exactly what his motive was.

In the meantime I only hoped that we could come to some satisfactory resolution for the family's sake that would make all of this worthwhile. Of course it would mean convincing Big Momma and Big Daddy to trust us again. After what had happened today, I wasn't sure they ever would. But I knew I would have to try.

I rinsed my hair, then climbed out of the water. Wrapped in a towel I paced the bathroom as I reminded myself that at least Maggie and Henry were happier, and that their relationship was back on track.

Something was nagging in the back of my head. It was like an itch I couldn't scratch. A feeling that I was missing something important. I had seen so many strange things since I had arrived here and I now found myself studying all the evidence again as the memories flicked through my mind like daguerreotype pictures of each scene.

I revisited the times I'd seen the form of Callon: an ink-black figure that had dripped glutinous ichor, and had looked as though he had been severely burned. He had smelt charred too and that awful odour followed whenever he had appeared. Even Sally, when questioned about her experience, had mentioned something about the smell of extinguished candles on the air. I hadn't thought it important at the time. Maybe it still wasn't.

A thought occurred to me. Perhaps we should set a trap for Callon this night. I needed to discuss this with Pepper and Martin.

In the bedroom, I slipped my breeches, shirt and a short red jacket on. I could feel a chill in the air since the storm, and with wet hair I wasn't sure if it would be wise to go outside without a coat of some sort.

Then I strapped on my weapons even though I had no idea what I was going to do, but if my theory was right, then I would find Callon walking the Plantation and right now I was the only eligible female in the house.

I opened up the curtains and slipped out onto the balcony. I was about to head to my colleagues' room when I changed my mind and went in the other direction.

I made my way silently down towards Maggie and Henry's room and listened at the door. All was quiet inside, and no light bled from around the drapes. I only hoped that they were now coming to terms with their differences and would start living the life of happiness they both deserved. The thought of helping them, above everything else, made what I was about to do crucial and my resolve strengthened, even though I felt that familiar rush of excitement and anxiety that precipitated a confrontation of this magnitude.

I walked back along the balcony towards Pepper and

Martin's room. I was about to knock on when I became aware of a presence behind me. I turned to find Orlando standing on the balcony outside my room.

'Boy, am I glad to see you,' I said. 'I've been wondering where you got to. Listen you need to know ...'

As I spoke, Orlando's features dissolved into the black mask of Callon and a powerful odour of charred flesh hit my nostrils.

'You can't win,' I said. 'We know everything now.'

The black face split into a wide but hideous grin. White teeth gleamed between burnt and cracked lips.

'The price wasn't paid,' rasped Callon and then his face sank, the image fading away into the shadows, and I found myself face to face with Maggie standing further down the balcony.

'That wasn't my brother ...' she gasped.

'No, that thing resembled him closely, and now has decided to mimic him. If it can do that, it can be anyone. Maggie you can't trust anyone now. Not until we have resolved this once and for all.'

Maggie wrung her hands. 'But what *can* you do? It's a demon. We can't fight it.'

'There's always a way to destroy a demon,' I said. 'You just need to learn their weaknesses. Then you use them to your own advantage.'

'What weakness does this one have?' Maggie asked.

'I don't know – yet. But at the moment it doesn't seem to have the strength to maintain his disguises for long. Anyway, you need to go back to your room and stay with Henry. That's the safest place for you right now.'

Maggie nodded. I saw her shadow fall over the balustrade as I turned around to walk towards Pepper and Martin's room.

I stopped.

Maggie also halted.

There was very little light on the balcony, certainly not enough to cast a shadow. As I swivelled back to look at her, I found Maggie smiling.

'Is something wrong, Kat?'

'You're ... *not* Maggie ...' I said slowly.

'Of course I am. At least, some of the time. She doesn't know that though, poor girl.'

'Callon.'

'That *is* a name I have used in recent years,' the voice that came from Maggie's lips had dropped in timbre and was no longer female, even though it came from her vocal cords.'

'How long have you been leaching on her?' I asked.

'Long enough,' Callon-Maggie said.

The penny was beginning to drop. Maggie was a conduit for this thing. It used her to link its soul to the real world, and while that link was intact, Callon could move around and search for ways in which to impregnate the women of the house with its half-breed spawn.

'I have been pretty naive,' I said. 'I guess I didn't see this coming at all. You're nothing without her. You don't even exist when she's away from the Plantation.'

'Perhaps ...' said the creature. 'But you did me a great favour today.'

'How so?'

'You've freed me. You broke the wards that were put on that room the night it was sealed.'

I was surprised that the creature would even give me this knowledge if it was such an important thing but it didn't take a genius to realise that he was merely enjoying gloating over his victory. I also knew that he was bluffing too. There were no wards on the room.

'If that's the case then you no longer need Maggie ...' I pointed out. 'So why don't you leave the poor girl in peace?'

Callon threw back Maggie's head and laughed through her mouth. It wasn't a pretty or female sound. It was more like a death rattle, it caught in her throat and lurked there, before breaking out between her lips in a witch's cackle.

'Well, that's where you will help me further,' said Callon. 'There is a small ritual that has to be performed to give me back my strength.'

'I doubt anyone on this Plantation will help you with that,' I said.

Callon grimaced in a way that was supposed to be a grin. I studied Maggie's body closely. Her eyes were wide. They darted around as though she were in a locked room trying to get out. He didn't have full control over her after all.

It was clear to me that Callon, despite his bravado, was still much weakened. Why that was I didn't know. Somehow in the past he'd had the strength to take form and seduce both

Big Momma and her younger sister. I suspected that the birth of Orlando had given him an even stronger foothold in the corporeal world. It must have been a tremendous blow when Isaac performed his ritual to remove the demon from Orlando.

'It was,' said Callon as though reading my thoughts. 'But I'm not the bad guy in all of this. The Pollitts cheated me. They failed to pay the forfeit.'

'But that was just one man,' I pointed out. 'Not the entire family. Not that I expect a demon like you to actual understand the idea of justice, or fair play ...'

Callon stopped trying to smile. 'I am no demon.'

'From where I'm standing you fit very well into that category.'

Maggie doubled over clutching her stomach as though she were in tremendous pain. I hurried to her side, hoping that somewhere inside her she had the strength to dispel the demon that had taken hold.

'Fight him, Maggie, no matter how much it hurts!'

Callon laughed again and Maggie straightened up. 'She can't fight me. She never could. She's as much my child as Orlando was before they ripped me outta him.'

'Miss Maggie?' said a voice behind her.

Callon-Maggie spun around to see that Isaac had now joined us on the balcony.

'Isaac,' I warned. 'It's not Maggie right now. Callon has her.'

Isaac ran his eyes over the head and shoulders of what looked to be Maggie and he took a step backwards.

'That ain't Callon in there ...' he said, his voice trembling.

Callon-Maggie began to laugh again and that awful gravelly sound issued from Maggie's body. It was like nails scratched on slate. The most grating sound and it vibrated in my soul as being pure and insane evil.

'*Daddy*?' said Isaac. 'You inside this poor girl?'

I thought for a moment that I had misheard Isaac. That what he said just couldn't be true. Callon wasn't, couldn't be, Isaac's father. How on earth was that even possible?

'*Daddy*? It *is* you!' he said again.

Callon-Maggie glared at Isaac as though he was affronted that the old man before him could ever confuse his demon soul with that of an old, long dead, voodoo priest.

'Whoever it is Isaac, we have to get him out of Maggie. Can you help?'

Isaac stepped forward and began to chant in that strange language I had heard him use in the clearing. The demon stepped back and then Maggie's body doubled over again and she groaned in pain, a sound that was more human than the awful laughter the creature had forced from Maggie's mortal throat.

I saw the thing release her, the shadow poured like black smoke from her eyes, nose and mouth. Maggie fell backwards against the wall of the house. I could see the demon now, a filthy miasma that exuded from her, but stayed connected by an ethereal umbilical cord.

I moved to go to her as she staggered, barely staying upright.

'Don't touch her none, Miss Kat,' Isaac said. 'She mighty

dangerous right now.'

He began to talk again in that guttural, high-pitched tongue and I knew he was addressing the thing that was attached to Maggie, trying to exorcise it from her. But as I watched I knew that Isaac's words were of no use. This thing was resisting him and it was tearing Maggie apart in the process.

Maggie's mouth was open in a silent scream, her face a mask of contorted pain while her limbs twisted and turned at unnatural angles.

'Stop it!' I said. 'You're killing her!'

By now Pepper, Martin and Henry had come from their rooms drawn by the noise. Henry tried to go to Maggie but Isaac held him back, issuing the same warning he had given to me. But the five of us fanned around her on the balcony, so that the demon couldn't force her to run and she, and it, was cornered.

'I can't fight my daddy with the magic he gave me. He already knows all the tricks and loop holes,' Isaac said. 'I can't hold it out of her for long, and I don't know how to separate it completely – not without ...'

'It will take her with it ...' I said.

'No!' gasped Henry as he tried once more to reach for his wife.

'Don't be a fool, man!' said Martin. 'You'll only make this worse!'

'Does someone want to get us up to speed,' Pepper said. 'What's this about Isaac's father?'

'Isaac thinks the demon is his father ... I *think* ...' I said.

'That's my daddy in there, it ain't no demon and I don't

knowed how this happen,' Isaac said. 'Daddy, let this poor girl go. What she gone done to you?'

When faced with a demon possession my usual reaction was to kill the body the monster possessed. But only when I felt certain that the human soul couldn't be saved. Those puzzle pieces were starting to fit again, this time in a way I found totally out of my comfort zone. If the demon was Isaac's father, a whole load of new questions were raised that I wasn't sure we would ever get answers to. The first one being, how the devil did this happen in the first place? The second, and most crucial of all, what could be done to put everything right?

Isaac began to chant again. Maggie stopped writhing and stood upright, pressing herself against the wall as though she were trying to escape the words that came from the houngan's lips.

'I taught you well, son,' she said. Then she closed her eyes and slumped to the floor.

This time when Henry moved to help his wife, Isaac didn't stop him.

'Let's get Miss Maggie back to her room,' said Isaac.

Pepper helped Henry lift her and they carried her back to her room and placed her on the bed.

'What the devil is going on?' asked Henry.

Isaac was shaken up, his brow was beaded with sweat and he didn't appear to be the confident character that I thought I had started to understand over the last few hours.

'Is she going to be all right?' Pepper asked.

'For now,' Isaac said. 'I used a sleeping spell weaved in

with a binding spell. She tied for now. He can't use her if'n she ain't able to move.'

Isaac was shaking so much I thought he would fall down. I took his arm and encouraged him down into a chair near the door.

'How'd I not knowed dis?' he said.

'How could you? He hid. None of us even suspected Maggie to be connected, we just thought she was his target, not his conduit.' I said. 'Isaac, what do you think happened here?'

'I don't know Miss Kat. I don't think I knows anything if I couldn't even see my own daddy was that thing all this time.'

'We know your father was involved in a ritual that separated Big Daddy from his demon-half. We know that your father disappeared after Master Pollitt failed to pay the forfeit. We know that Orlando was the son of this thing that calls itself Callon. We know that you performed the same ritual on him, as your father performed on Big Daddy,' Martin said.

'Summarising isn't getting us anywhere,' Pepper said. 'We need to learn what happened to Isaac's father, maybe then we will understand how he became Callon.'

'I was getting to that,' said Martin. 'We know that both Big Daddy and Orlando were born twinned with sisters. In each case none of the girls were suspected of having any demon blood. But it appears now that Maggie is somehow attached to this thing. It's been feeding off her energy, using her to ground itself in this reality.'

'Yes ...' I sighed. 'So?'

'Every time Maggie was absent, so was this thing …?' Martin asked looking directly at Isaac.

'Yes,' Isaac nodded.

'It was always with her. And she was never its intended victim. She was being used to give it access. It's like a … leech. Instead of feeding on her blood, it was feeding on her soul,' Martin said.

'Does this mean that something is also attached to Big Daddy's sister?' I asked trying to follow Martin's line of thinking.

'I think it unlikely. I think this wasn't supposed to happen. I suspect that the demon who fathered Big Daddy is long gone. It probably passed through, somehow seduced his pregnant mother, Lacey, leaving it's nephilim child to find a home in this world. The intervention of your father, Isaac, changed the process that was supposed to happen. Then, there was the unpaid sacrifice for the magic used … Have you ever had a situation like that occur before?'

'Nobody is dumb enough to not pay. I never seen anything go wrong before, but my daddy said there would be consequences. Masser Pollitt was cursed for it, no doubt.'

'Well, it's time to find out the truth from the only person likely to know,' I said.

'Who?' asked Pepper. 'Master Pollitt and his wife are long dead.'

'Yes. But Big Daddy knew something. He was pretty upset about us uncovering his old bedroom. And I don't think it was just because of the damage we did either.'

21

A pale glow of artificial light brightened the end of the corridor on the right wing. The light was coming from the room we had uncovered.

Carrying a lamp to light our way, I led Martin and Pepper past our rooms and down towards the opening.

As we reached the new doorway, the light inside grew brighter. I paused at the threshold, recalling the previous times I had crossed it, not in this world, but into some other and the small boy, whose demon-half was caught there. A child that didn't seem to me to be deserving of his fate.

'This is where it happened,' said Big Daddy from inside the room.

He was sitting on the edge of the bed gazing around the dusty room like a sleep-walker who had just woken to find himself in the middle of a real-life nightmare.

The three of us stepped inside.

Big Daddy looked a broken man. His complexion – no longer the ruddy cheerful, slightly plump man he had seemed when we arrived – was gaunt and yellowed. He looked sick, and I felt that tremendous guilt again. What right had we to come into their lives and completely destroy them with our curiosity? Surely the Pollitts were dealing with their haunting, even if it hadn't been effectively?

I quickly realised this was all silly and unnecessary remorse however. Maggie and Henry had been suffering and now that we knew that Callon was controlling Maggie, the situation had become untenable. We had to finish whatever it was that we started.

Now Big Daddy sat before us studying his trembling hands, and I felt a sense of anticipation as I waited for the explanation that would finally solve this mystery – the last piece being placed in the most difficult and challenging puzzle we had ever been faced with.

'What happened?' I asked.

'This is where I died,' said Big Daddy. 'This is where they ripped me apart, and put me back together again.'

'We know about the ritual,' Martin said.

'What we don't know,' I said, 'is what happened to Isaac's father.'

Big Daddy glanced up sharply. 'What does this have to do with him?'

'It has everything to do with him,' I said. 'I'll explain why, but you need to tell us the truth.'

Big Daddy shrugged. 'You said you know of the ritual.

What do you want me to tell you? How it hurt so much I thought I was dying? How I felt every rip and tear as they prised it from my soul? How that by removing the Darkness they left me as only half a man, always feeling like part of me was missing? How, even though I knew this, I subjected my son Orlando to the same pain?'

'I'm sorry,' I said. 'It was perhaps not the right thing to do, but the demon in you was potentially evil. It could have hurt those around you. You tried to drown your sister, and later Orlando did the same. I don't see what choice your father had, or that you had for that matter. You couldn't leave Orlando that way, could you?'

'Yes. I could have. Orlando didn't try to drown Amelia. It was Maggie. I saw it, but I didn't want to blame her, and I hated my son. I resented that he was whole while I was not. I didn't know though, that after the ritual was performed I would feel such remorse that I could barely look him in the eyes anymore.'

'Maggie tried to kill Amelia?' I said, realising despite the newly acquired knowledge of Maggie's state, that this had never occurred to me at all.

Big Daddy nodded.

'And you didn't try to drown your own sister?' Pepper asked.

'No. I loved her. Why would I ever do that?'

'This is worse than I thought,' I said. 'A terrible travesty has been done to both of you. And I would have been just as guilty of committing it as anyone would have been. I've always believed that nephilims were evil.'

'Nephilim?' Big Daddy said.

'Yes. That's what you are … were. The child of demon and human parents.'

'It stands to reason,' said Pepper, 'that the human part of a soul has as much chance of being the dominant party as the demon one does. It seems so obvious now that it is put before us this way.'

'What appears to be a monster, doesn't have to be one. It has freedom of choice, just like anyone does,' Martin concluded.

Big Daddy's eyes lowered again. He was sad enough already and we just had to keep breaking his heart even more. He began to talk then, and the tale he told brought everything together in a neat little bow that went a long way to breaking more hearts, but would help, in the long run, to heal them too.

'My daddy killed Matthias, Isaac's father.

'It was a few nights after the ritual had been done. I was here, in my room, when Matthias came in. He told me something bad had been done to me. Something he'd been party to with the best of intentions. "Masser Pollitt done us both wrong," he said. "And now the magic has to be appeased."

'Matthias told me he was going to reverse the spell. That I'd be "whole" again and the choices I made in life would be down to my soul, complete as it would be. I didn't really understand it all. All I knew was that I'd been punished for something I hadn't done. I knew it all along, but no one would listen to me.

'As Matthias began his sing-song chanting, my daddy came into the room with six of the overseers. They caught hold of the servant and they began to beat him. One of them, a man called Edward Brewster, tried to stop another from smashing the butt of the rifle into Matthias's face. He was a kindly man I remember, and often intervened when the other white employees were too tough on the blacks. But Brewster was pulled aside by two others and the overseer finished what he started. I saw Matthias's jaw crumple, blood burst from his nose, and he spat out several teeth, but still he tried to say those strange words, to complete what he had started.

'For trying to stop the brutality Brewster was shot in the back of the head by my daddy. His body fell at the foot of my bed, even as his blood and skull splattered over the bedspread.

'I cowered in my bed, but I felt Matthias's magic beginning to work and that demon coming back to where it belonged in the centre of my body, right by my heart.

'With Brewster dead, the men beat on Matthias some more. One of them kicked him between the legs, that stopped him talking right enough, and he was heaving and sick all over the rug with the pain it caused. The man's eyes were so swelled up by then they were almost closed shut. I heard limbs breaking as those men continued to hit him, and I pulled the covers up over my head so that I couldn't hear and see any more of it.

'After a while they dragged him from the room, along with Brewster, who didn't deserve anything like that to happen to him either.

'I climbed out of my bed and went over to the window and saw them starting a fire, right where the lawn is now. Matthias's body was thrown on it like a broken effigy. He laid there in the flames for a while and the smell of burnt flesh wafted up towards me. Matthias, despite his broken body, tried to pull himself from those flames though. That man had a will to live, and he wanted to put this all right again. I knew he did.

'As he fell from that bonfire, the men doused him with pails of water, then they dragged his body off somewhere else.

'After a while my daddy came back and he took me out of this room and put me over in the wing on the other side of the house. Right next door to him and my momma. I never saw this room again, or any of the things I had in it. But the next day, I found a team of men over in the right wing, and they were decorating the landing so that it covered over the door. My room vanished overnight. Inside and outside, like it never existed.

'The house slaves were changed a few days later. My father separated them all from the others at first, and then fearing that somehow they'd pass on the news of what they saw, he sent each and every one of them away. He didn't want the other slaves to learn about the death of Matthias. He knew that they followed him, and his voodoo religion. I heard it said that they were all sold off at the next auctions.

'After that we got a whole group of new ones that didn't know there had ever been that extra room because they had never been allowed inside the house before.

'Also, rumours were put about that Matthias had run away and that he'd killed one of the overseers in the process. All the slaves were made to attend Brewster's funeral. And they did so gladly as he was the only one of the white overseers that had ever been kind to them.

'But it didn't end there. I was given to nightmares after that. I saw Matthias, charred blacker than his skin could ever be walking the land like a lost soul. Sometimes when I was playing outside, I even saw him on the balcony, right outside where my window and door had once been. But he couldn't come inside the house and as I grew up, I saw him less and less until I completely forgot that he had ever existed.'

When his tale ended I felt sad for the boy that Big Daddy had once been. He had grown up in a house that had a curse on it. Although we now knew that Matthias had somehow become Callon, a demon that haunted Pollitt land, and how he had died, we still did not know *how* this voodoo priest had turned into the vengeful demon. The reason why he sought revenge was blatantly obvious though.

'So you don't know where they hid Matthias' body?' I said.

Big Daddy shook his head.

'You see if we find the remains, we may be able to put this man finally to rest,' Martin explained.

It was interesting that although Isaac had been unable to recognise his father behind the veneer of Callon, Big Daddy had, on some level, known that the demon was Matthias. Even so, he didn't know that Matthias was able to take on human form in order to gain entry to the house, and to exact his revenge on the family by creating another nephilim child that he would use to punish the family.

Big Daddy, though he was clearly consumed with guilt, had nothing to blame himself for however. He had been a child at the time, and had also treated the slaves well once he inherited the Plantation.

'I could never stomach beatings or mistreatment after seeing what had happened to Matthias,' Big Daddy said. 'No man deserved that. And when the time came, and Isaac wanted freedom for all, I was willing to pay the price, even though I was unhappy about putting Orlando through that same torment I'd experienced as a child and never forgotten. That's why it took me so long to commit to it. Not because I didn't want to free the slaves, that to me wasn't the sacrifice at all. Hurting my son was.'

We left Big Daddy alone in the room and went back to Henry's room to see how Maggie was doing. By now I was feeling totally exhausted, and could think of nothing more than crawling into my own bed and sleeping until noon, but the night wasn't done and we had to come up with something that would help us end this torment once and for all.

'My daddy deserved revenge,' Isaac said when we explained what had happened to him.

I was concerned that he'd become angry with Big

Daddy, even though I saw him as much a victim in this as Matthias was.

'But it ain't Big Daddy's fault,' Isaac said. 'And his spirit has wronged this family for the sins of another man. I ain't of the belief that the sins of a father should be visited on his children. That ain't justice. And I don't think my daddy, if'n he were living would see it this way either. Somehow he got caught up on his death with the magic that should have been reversed. It's been trying to undo the damage ever since.'

I had to agree that the situation was a bad one for all concerned. I asked Isaac if he could return the other half of Big Daddy's soul to him, and indeed Orlando's. I was surprised at myself for even suggesting it. It meant the return of possible evil to both men, and could have a devastating effect on their lives. They may not be the good people they were now. They might, instead, become something that I would feel obliged to kill and I didn't relish being in that position but it seemed like the right thing to do.

Of course this wouldn't solve the immediate problem we had with Maggie.

'It might though, Miss Kat,' Isaac said. 'If we return Big Daddy's soul, the magic will be happy. The forfeit will be no longer needed. It may just free my daddy to move onto the next world. And then he might let go of Miss Maggie.'

'Can you do the ritual tonight?' I asked.

'Yessum. I will just have to go and get some things. We will need Big Daddy to be willing, and it will have to be done in that room.

Pepper went with Isaac to fetch what was needed, and Martin and I went back to the room to pose the suggestion to Big Daddy. Much to our surprise Big Daddy agreed immediately.

As I waited in the room for the others to make their preparations and join me, I shivered. Demon hunting might be what I did now, but it didn't mean I had to like it.

22

For his comfort, I took the throw from my room and I placed it over the dusty, blood stained covers before Big Daddy lay down on the bed while Isaac set up the tools for his ritual.

'It's a little different to what you seen before,' Isaac explained. 'Because we are reversing what was done. There shouldn't be any pain this time, but I can' promise nothin.''

Big Daddy nodded. 'I'm sorry about your daddy,' he said with tears in his eyes.

'It ain't your fault,' Isaac reassured him. 'I only hope I can undo what damage done and you can all move on with your lives. Vengeance she be the worst evil. It eats at men's souls and feeds the Darkness. My daddy knew that, but ... that old evil got him anyway.'

'Whatever happens I promise we'll try and find his remains,' Big Daddy said.

Isaac said nothing, but he daubed some strong smelling

oil on Big Daddy's forehead, then across his now bared chest, and finally on the souls of his feet and the palms of his hands. Then he asked Big Daddy to stretch out his arms and legs into the shape of a star.

After that he poured salt in a large circle around the bed, and we placed lit candles wherever Isaac directed. I had never taken part in any form of magic ceremony and I felt a little uncomfortable with the whole proceedings but I was determined to see this through, and then, if need be, help with the reversal on Orlando too. Part of me was interested in what kind of man that would make him once he was given a choice to be good or bad. Would I, for example, be able to sense the demon in him?

When the formalities were addressed, Isaac asked us all to stay out of the salt circle. He said it was important that none of us crossed inside during the rite until he told us it was safe. He also remained outside.

'We're going to be bringing demon energy into the circle, to re-bond with Big Daddy. We really don' wan' that to go into the wrong person,' Isaac explained.

The three of us promised to stay back, no matter what we saw, and we took up positions around the bed, but well back from the circle's edge. I was placed with my back to the corridor, while Pepper was beside Isaac at the other side of the bed and Martin was at the foot.

The proceedings began and Isaac started to talk once more in his high, then low pitched tongue. I glanced at Pepper and Martin in turn to see what they made of it all but both

214

men were keeping their expressions deliberately blank.

Almost immediately a whoosh of energy rippled through the atmosphere, and the circle around Big Daddy seemed to undulate like the air coming from a hot furnace. I felt heat on my face and I glanced over at Isaac to see it this was what was supposed to happen.

All I could see were the whites of his eyes, the dark brown irises had completely disappeared, as though his eyes had rolled backwards into his head. His face was blank and his skin looked waxy as sweat burst out over his features. He continued to chant and his hand raised up his bone shard-covered staff, shaking it towards the figure on the bed.

I looked back at Big Daddy. He was lying still but his eyes were wide open and he seemed afraid.

'The portal is open,' Isaac said in English just as I saw a shift in the atmosphere inside the circle.

I saw once more the little boy that had been Big Daddy. He turned his head and looked at me, startled, and I realised that he could see us. He seemed afraid as the two realities began to overlap like multiple reflections in a pool of water. The same, but different.

'It's all right!' I called to him taking a step closer.

'Kat!' called Martin, and I halted, realising what I had almost done.

I stepped back again. The boy had heard me though and he lay down on his bed, his small figure glowing and overlapping with the body of Big Daddy.

Isaac's chanting became more insistent and I saw the

two worlds merging for a moment.

Then there was an almighty scream from the doorway.

I turned to see Maggie running forward towards the bed, and I fell in her path. We grappled, but she had the strength of several insane men. I was tossed aside, but I caught her foot, tumbling her down.

I fell over her, trying to hold her, even as Pepper and Martin hurried around the circle to help me restrain her.

I felt the touch of Callon's cord between us. The shadow loomed by the doorway, but didn't seem to be able or willing to enter the room.

'We're trying to help you!' I said. 'Can't you see that?'

Maggie wriggled beneath me, and started to crawl towards the circle. I joined both of my hands together to make a club, and hit her hard on the back of the neck. She collapsed forward, her body crumpling briefly. Then as I released my hold on her she suddenly revived and tried to crawl forward once more. By this time Pepper and Martin had reached us. The two men pulled her up, but she struggled and almost got free of them. I knew they wouldn't be able to hold onto her, but didn't know what to do. I only hoped that the ceremony would end soon.

During this time Isaac continued to chant, and fortunately was not distracted from the rite at all by the battle that was happening in the room.

Maggie pulled one arm free from Pepper's grasp, she was as slippery as an eel, but Pepper caught hold of her again.

'Your knife, Kat,' he said, desperately trying to hold on.

'I can't kill her!'

'No. It's silver. Cut. The. Cord,' Martin said though he could barely talk with the exertion.

I pulled my knife from my boot, and prayed that this would work to at least temporarily disconnect Callon with Maggie.

From the doorway Callon growled like a wolf about to pounce. I didn't look at him though, because I felt certain that without Maggie he was defenceless. I blinked and looked down at Maggie's stomach. I could see the faint curl of the ectoplasmic line. I swung the knife and much to my surprise, I felt it bite, as though the cord were more corporeal than ethereal after all.

Maggie screamed as though she were in tremendous pain and slumped in the arms of my colleagues. I looked over my shoulder and saw Callon's shadow shrinking backwards. I hurried to the door. The shadow fell from one side of the landing to the other, like a staggering man who had indulged in too much wine. Then it disappeared around the corner.

I turned back to survey the room. Martin and Pepper had laid the prone figure of Maggie down on the floor as far away from the salt circle as possible.

A few moments later the vibrating, hot air inside the circle glowed brightly and Big Daddy grunted, took in a breath and then gave a deep sigh. The circle of heat fell. The chant stopped. Isaac had finished.

I found I was leaning against the splintered opening, my breath ragged from the effort of the tussle I'd had with Maggie.

The brightness from the circle had extinguished, plummeting the room back to the candlelit gloom it had been earlier. Isaac remained where he was for a moment, though his illegible mantra had ceased. He closed his white eyes, and a moment later, when he opened them, they were normal again. Then he stepped across the salt line and helped Big Daddy to sit up.

Big Daddy opened his own eyes. They were now glowing a bright yellow instead of blue.

'It worked,' I said.

'How do you feel?' asked Pepper kindly.

'Whole. I can feel ... something dark ... inside me, but ... I am too long in the tooth and too set in my ways to let this thing change me for the worst. Strangely I feel ... more love and compassion than I did before. I have ... an understanding of the good things I've done, that weren't so much choices, as defaults. I'm glad I did them and feel I still would choose to take those paths. But until now, something inside me has always been ... cold.'

I listened, hoping that what he was saying was genuine, but part of me remained wary. It was in my nature to be cautious of anything with demon blood. The reach of the Darkness was everywhere. I only hoped that Big Daddy was right about his self control. After all he still had his human side, and didn't all of us have to make choices about taking right and wrong paths in life? Why should he be any different?

Martin and Pepper carried Maggie back to her room, where we found Henry waking with a nasty bump on his head. Maggie had hit him when his back was turned.

'Is she all right?' he asked, struggling to his feet and hurrying to her side.

'I don't know. She suffered an almighty shock. We had to use desperate means to sever her from Callon.

Henry tucked her back up in bed while Isaac went out to send someone to fetch a doctor to see Maggie. Pepper opted to stay with Henry in case she woke again and this wasn't over. In the meantime, the rest of us planned to try and get some sleep.

23

I returned to my room, exhaustion both emotional and physical weighed heavily on my mind, body and soul. I was about to remove my clothing once more when I noticed the door leading to the balcony was slightly ajar.

As I reached it, the door opened and I found Orlando standing there.

'Is this *really* you?' I asked. 'Only we've played this scenario a few times this evening and I'm getting tired of it.'

'Miss Kat, whatever do you mean?'

I touched his arm, found him to be solid enough and I sighed with both relief and exhaustion.

'Sorry,' I said. 'It's been a long night.'

'I just saw my father, he told me what had happened,' Orlando said.

I nodded. 'I'm willing to talk to you about this Orlando, but I'm absolutely exhausted. Can we pick this up tomorrow?

I really need to just go to bed.'

Orlando frowned. His yellow eyes seemed brighter in the gaslight than in natural daylight and I found his scrutiny unnerving. Also, just walking into my room like that wasn't a very gentlemanly thing to do. If I had learnt anything about Orlando, it was that he addressed propriety at all times, and was deeply respectful towards me and everyone else. Never once, in the time since we had met, had I actually felt under threat. Until now.

'You're not Orlando …' I realised. 'You're him.'

'I'm both,' he said. A smile broke across his face revealing teeth too sharp to be held in a human mouth.'

I pulled my Perkins-Armley from its holster and pointed it as Orlando advanced and I retreated.

'You've been a thorn in my side since you arrived,' he said.

'I suppose I'm talking to Callon now? Don't you get it? The ritual was reversed. There's no sacrifice to pay anymore.'

'This ain't about no forfeit. I tol' Isaac that magic had to be paid for. It ain't strickly true that it will curse those who don't hold to their bargain. But that white man betrayed me, then destroyed my body and left my soul in torment. Have you any idea how it feels to be able to see your family and friends. You talk – they don't hear you. Your own son doesn't recognise you … Your wife ups and marries your best friend and goes on to sprout more offspring, year on year. I could see it all. I knowed what was happenin.'

'I'm sorry. But I'm finding it hard to have sympathy for a demon that sent a poor young girl so mad she had to be hospitalized. Or seduced a pregnant woman so that you could implant your own spawn inside her. What you've done was wrong, Callon. Or should I call you Matthias?'

'Matthias is dead. Callon is who I am now.'

I searched Orlando's body for any sign of an external joining with Callon's spirit, but I could see nothing like the cord that had been attached to Maggie. Maybe this was a straightforward case of possession but I hoped it wasn't because that would probably mean I would have to kill him – and I really didn't want to.

I suppose I should have wondered about my sudden sentiment but I didn't. It was cut and dried and straightforward that I would have to kill the demon-possessed body of a person when I didn't know them. But I had come to quite like Orlando in the few short days we had been at the Plantation and this wasn't going to be easy.

'How did you manage to take Orlando so easily?' I said.

Callon laughed. 'Isaac did a real good job on him. He emptied Orlando out so much that any demon coulda walked right inside …'

I backed towards the door that led to the hallway, ready to shout for help. Maybe Pepper and Martin would help me capture him. And maybe Isaac would find a way to remove Callon without hurting Orlando.

Suddenly Orlando-Callon leapt forward, knocking my gun from my hand as he reached for me. My Perkins-Armley fell to the floor and skittered under the bed. I ducked down, falling forward into a roll that would bring me back up on my feet, out of reach and near the balcony door. The roll went to plan and the demon stumbled clumsily, almost losing his balance while I was already on my feet and running towards the door. Fortunately as I came back to my feet I saw my Remington-Crewe lying on the floor. I grabbed it, realising it must have been there since the night Callon tried to suffocate me. I almost kissed the barrel of this loved and trusted laser weapon. Somehow it always found its way back into my hands: just the same as it had in the warehouse when I thought it had gone for good.

One thing was certain, a demon-possessed body was slow. They had to take time to feel comfortable with the height, build and the way the limbs moved before they could properly control it. This worked to my advantage because Orlando's body was newly possessed.

I holstered the gun then ran out onto the balcony, climbed up onto the balustrade and leapt off towards the airship without even thinking.

I collided with the canvas balloon, fingers scrabbling at the ropes, even as I began to slide off and downwards. The curve of the balloon aided me, had it been round and not the shape of a huge bullet, I might have fallen. As it was, I curved my body round it until I managed to gain purchase.

Once I'd found one I scrabbled down and underneath the balloon until I could drop down on the deck. But my attempts to escape from Orlando-Callon had completely failed. I had not banked on him adapting to the body so quickly. While I was struggling to hold onto the balloon, the creature had already jumped down from the balcony onto the deck.

As I landed, bent-kneed on the shiny metal surface, Callon was waiting for me.

I tried to fool him again, but this time he was ready when I feigned right, then went left. He caught hold of me by the collar of my jacket and then slipped his hands around my neck.

I threw myself back, shoulder blades connecting with the wheel, then I rolled, pulling Callon-Orlando with me. But the creature was strong and instead of shaking him free I felt his hands slip around my throat as he yanked me back towards him.

I felt the air cut from my lungs immediately and experienced the terrible pain of impending suffocation. My lungs felt as though they would burst in my chest as he slowly crushed my throat. I propelled myself backwards. This time I felt the control panel of the airship up against my back. The hard levers pressed into my shoulders and spine, and then suddenly the two engines, either side of the balloon, burst into life with a loud roar.

Callon-Orlando was briefly distracted. Using the pressure against the controls as leverage, I pulled up both knees between us and used the strength of my legs to kick out and propel the monster away. He stumbled backwards as the airship tilted and jerked.

I slumped to my knees gasping in a lungful of air and, as Callon-Orlando regained his footing, I pulled the Remington-Crewe free of the holster and fired. The laser hissed, but failed to fire. I glanced down at the SunPan and realised that the gun had not been recharged since I last used it.

Callon-Orlando was on me again. Fingers ferociously clamped once more around my already bruised throat. My hands beat at him to no avail: he was just too strong, and then, as a roaring sound filled my ears and I felt I was on the brink of collapse I remembered the crossbow that was still hanging from my weapon belt.

My hands stopped their efforts to push Orlando away and groped instead for the crossbow. Fortunately I always kept it fully wound and loaded but with the safety catch on to avoid accidental firing. There was no time to release the hook that held it to my belt, instead I just turned the weapon between us, released the safety and fired a round of silver plated arrows straight into Orlando's body.

Orlando fell back, blood blossomed on the front of his crisp white shirt as he stared at me, shocked and in pain and very much himself again.

'Miss Kat,' he gasped.

I pulled myself up into a sitting position. I heard yelling, felt the tug of someone climbing up the rope ladder on the starboard bow.

The airship rocked and twisted, the engines still firing, and I felt certain that it would pull free of the mooring ropes if I didn't turn them off.

I staggered to my feet, one hand still holding the crossbow, the other going to my bruised throat. I gasped in air, but felt dizzy as I stumbled towards the control panel. Then, before I could reach the controls I fell into an uncharacteristic faint brought on by the sudden rush of blood and air to my brain.

I awoke to find Pepper looking into my face with a look of deep concern.

'Thank God!' he said. 'She's coming to …'

The metal deck was hot against my back. I struggled to sit up and Pepper helped me to my feet, but kept his arm firmly around my waist. Only then did I notice that the crossbow had been prised from my fingers, and was no longer attached to my belt.

'What happened?' I asked.

'We were about to ask you that. It seems you've killed Orlando,' Martin said kneeling down beside the body.

I looked over at the corpse of the ill-fated nephilim and allowed the tears to flow unchecked as I sobbed uncontrollably. Martin looked away from the sight of me falling apart. I could see he was embarrassed. They had never seen any weakness in me and I couldn't explain at all why I was so upset. I wasn't sure who I was crying for most, me or Orlando. I was intensely sad that another poor innocent had been lost to the Darkness. I could no longer deny the friendship that had been blossoming between us, even though I knew it had been nothing more than that. I would miss him. And just this once I wanted to *save* a possessed soul, not send it on to whatever dimension it deserved to go to: be that a heaven or a hell. I hoped for Orlando's sake that it was the former.

I still felt weak and sick, my vision was blurred, and so I let Pepper help me over to look at the body. Holding onto Pepper steadied my nerves and dried my tears. He was always my rock and I realised at that moment that he was also more than a friend to me.

'Callon possessed him,' I explained. 'I had no choice.'

Martin nodded. 'I'll fetch Isaac. A bad result, but I think this is finally over.'

Epilogue

The Pollitts had their own cemetery some distance from the house. A modest graveyard surrounding a small family chapel. It was a bright sunny day as they lowered the body of Orlando into the ground, and the priest said the words of internment.

I felt saddened for the family, but a quiet relief seemed to follow the initial grief when the realisation that their terrible persecution was at an end.

This was the second funeral to take place here that week. The first was that of the charred remains of Isaac's father, Matthias, which the voodoo priest found after casting a location spell. Matthias had been inside Big Daddy's old bedroom all along, buried in the cavity that had once been the door leading to the balcony.

Big Daddy had insisted that the man be given a decent burial, but he let Isaac preside over the proceedings and respected their religious beliefs which we all hoped would ensure that Matthias would stay at peace this time. Isaac said that he was. His soul had been taken on to whatever realm it deserved to reside in – never more to cast an evil shadow over the lives of the Pollitts.

There had been questions asked. No one cried more than Big Momma over the death of Orlando, but she didn't seem to hold it against us nonetheless when the facts were made clear.

Maggie was better too. She and Henry held hands all the way through the service and afterwards, when they thought no one was looking as they walked away from the grave, Henry placed a loving kiss on her welcoming lips. They were going to be all right. I just knew it.

After the funeral, Pepper, Martin and I climbed aboard the tin-covered airship. I was keen to return to New York and our own life, and even though I felt that I needed a rest from it all, I knew I would always be ready to face the Darkness in any of its forms. And so, as quietly as possible, we took to the skies and turned the airship away from Pollitt Plantation.

On the journey back, as Martin demonstrated his new improvements – the two engines I'd accidentally set off were run by a powerful jet that forced air through them and propelled the airship faster through the sky; a hidden harpoon gun that ejected from the hull of the ship; and a row of lights that lit the interior with energy sourced from the sun panels – I turned to find Pepper watching me. His eyes were warm, they held a light that I had on occasion noticed, but had often chosen to ignore.

I was ready to move on now. Ready to start living.

I smiled at Pepper. And my expression said: *Yes. I like you. Yes, you are my friend. Yes, you could be something more.*

Or at least I hoped it did.

ZOMBIES IN NEW YORK
AND OTHER BLOODY JOTTINGS
By SAM STONE

Something is sapping the energy of the usually robust dancers of the Moulin Rouge … Zombies roam the streets of New York City … Clowns die in mysteriously humorous ways … Jack the Ripper's crimes are investigated by a vampire …

Welcome to the horrific and poetic world of Sam Stone, where Angels are stalking the undead and a vampire becomes obsessed with a centuries-old werewolf. Terror and lust go hand in hand in the disturbing world of the Toymaker, and the haunting Siren's call draws the hapless further into a waking nightmare.

THIRTEEN STORIES OF HORROR AND PASSION, AND SIX MYTHOLOGICAL AND EROTIC POEMS FROM THE PEN OF THE NEW QUEEN OF VAMPIRE FICTION.

Contains the 2011 British Fantasy Award Winning short story 'Fool's Gold'.

Available now in Paperback, Audio and Ebook

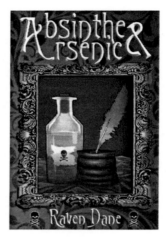

DOCTOR TRIPPS: KAIJU COCKTAIL
By KIT COX

After dropping a devastating bomb on London Docklands, Dr Tripps goes underground for twelve years while he formulates an evil plan to destroy diesel technology. With the help of a mermaid and a fly-monkey butler he devises a mysterious cocktail.

Meanwhile a young engineer, mistaken for his master and drawn into a mysterious, old and very secret society becomes an unlikely hero.

In London, the NANI agency sends out their newest recruit, Nanny Honey, to protect the children of the Russian Tsar.

As Tripps' Kaiju Cocktail is fed out into the world, weird and devastating mutations begin to occur that threaten the very fabric of society.

A NEOVICTORIAN WORLD WHERE STEAM IS PITTED AGAINST DIESEL, BUT WHICH SIDE WILL WIN?

Available now in Paperback and Ebook

SPECTRE
By STEPHEN LAWS

The inseparable Byker Chapter: six boys, one girl, growing up together in the back streets of Newcastle.

Now memories are all that Richard Eden has left, and one treasured photograph. But suddenly, inexplicably, the images of his friends start to fade, and as they vanish, so his friends are found dead and mutilated.

Something is stalking the Chapter, picking them off one by one, something connected with their past, and with the girl they used to know.

'The plot is brilliant, the writing superb. It's absolutely terrifying – a living nightmare' *Starburst*

The book is an authors' preferred edition, featuring reinstated material and a new afterword by the author.

Available now in Paperback and Ebook

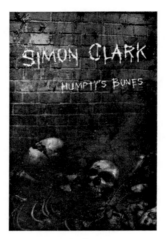

RULES OF DUEL
By GRAHAM MASTERTON
and WILLIAM S BURROUGHS

Depressed reporter Tom Crisp, sometimes known as A14, finds himself embroiled in a web of intrigue as he tries to make sense of his incarceration at Tin Type Hall. 'Just telling you' his story unravels in a series of 'silver film' as he finds himself in a world full of double-agents such as the psychotic Motherwell the Everlasting Executioner, John Remorse, the Serjeant of Time Film and Samuel Baptist HM Inspector of Brothels.

In a world where sexually charged sofas ejaculate black horse hair and the Hypocritic Oath is blamed for failed medical procedures, Crisp stands helplessly by as Jack Beauregard, the Eater of Cities, is hunted down.

It could all be the fault of the Mysterious Babies … but then maybe you can feel the 'Cold Sun'…

Graham Masterton wrote *Rules of Duel* between 1964 and 1970, when he was friends with William S Burroughs, the creator of the literarily acclaimed intersection writing technique. Recently rediscovered, this is a thought-provoking, triumphant and poetic tribute to Burroughs. *Rules of Duel* is a clever and pervasive novel, which turns literature on its head, and makes the reader work to be part of the evolving plot. Complete with original introduction by Burroughs, written before his death in 1997, *Rules of Duel* is a previously unpublished masterpiece from two of the greatest writers of their generations.

Available now in Paperback and Ebook

URBAN GOTHIC: LACUNA AND OTHER TRIPS edited by
DAVID J HOWE
Tales of horror from and inspired by the *Urban Gothic* television
series. Contributors: Graham Masterton, Christopher Fowler, Simon
Clark, Steve Lockley & Paul Lewis, Paul Finch and Debbie Bennett.

KING OF ALL THE DEAD by STEVE LOCKLEY & PAUL LEWIS
The king of all the dead will have what is his.

THE HUMAN ABSTRACT by GEORGE MANN
A future tale of private detectives, AIs, Nanobots, love and death.

BREATHE by CHRISTOPHER FOWLER
The Office meets *Night of the Living Dead*.

HOUDINI'S LAST ILLUSION by STEVE SAVILE
Can the master illusionist Harry Houdini outwit the dead shades of
his past?

ALICE'S JOURNEY BEYOND THE MOON by R J CARTER
A sequel to the classic Lewis Carroll tales.

APPROACHING OMEGA by ERIC BROWN
A colonisation mission to Earth runs into problems.

VALLEY OF LIGHTS by STEPHEN GALLAGHER
A cop comes up against a body-hopping murderer.

PRETTY YOUNG THINGS by DOMINIC MCDONAGH
A nest of lesbian rave bunny vampires is at large in Manchester.
When Chelsey's ex-boyfriend is taken as food, Chelsey has to get
out fast.

A MANHATTAN GHOST STORY by T M WRIGHT
Do you see ghosts? A classic tale of love and the supernatural.

SHROUDED BY DARKNESS: TALES OF TERROR edited by
ALISON L R DAVIES
An anthology of tales guaranteed to bring a chill to the spine. This
collection has been published to raise money for DebRA, a national
charity working on behalf of people with the genetic skin blistering
condition, Epidermolysis Bullosa (EB). Featuring stories by: Debbie
Bennett, Poppy Z Brite, Simon Clark, Storm Constantine, Peter
Crowther, Alison L R Davies, Paul Finch, Christopher Fowler,
Neil Gaiman, Gary Greenwood, David J Howe, Dawn Knox, Tim
Lebbon, Charles de Lint, Steven Lockley & Paul Lewis, James
Lovegrove, Graham Masterton, Richard Christian Matheson,
Justina Robson, Mark Samuels, Darren Shan and Michael Marshall
Smith. With a frontispiece by Clive Barker and a foreword by
Stephen Jones. Deluxe hardback cover by Simon Marsden.

BLACK TIDE by DEL STONE JR
A college professor and his students find themselves trapped by an
encroaching horde of zombies following a waste spillage.

FORCE MAJEURE by DANIEL O'MAHONY
An incredible fantasy novel. Kay finds herself trapped in a strange
city in the Andes ... a place where dreams can become reality, and
where dragons may reside.

TELOS PUBLISHING
Email: orders@telos.co.uk
Web: www.telos.co.uk

To order copies of any Telos books, please visit our website where
there are full details of all titles and facilities for worldwide credit
card online ordering, as well as occasional special offers.